THE GARDEN OF JOYS

Works by Henry Cattan

Jerusalem, Saqi Books, London, 2000

The Palestine Question, Saqi Books, London, 2000

The Evolution of Oil Concessions in the Middle East and North Africa, Oceana Publications for Parker School of Foreign and Comparative Law, New York, 1967

The Law of Oil Concessions in the Middle East and North Africa, Oceana Publications, New York, 1967

To Whom Does Palestine Belong?, Bouheiry Brothers, Beirut, 1967

Palestine, the Arabs and Israel, Longman, London, 1969 and 1970

Palestine, the Road to Peace, Longman, London, 1970

Palestine and International Law, Longman, London, 1973, 1974 and 1976

The Question of Jerusalem, Third World Centre for Research and Publishing, London, 1980

The Solution of the Palestine Refugee Problem, International Progress Organization, Vienna, 1982

Le jardin des joies, Gaston Lachurie, Paris, 1985

The Garden of Joys

An Anthology of Oriental Anecdotes,
Fables and Proverbs

Translated and related by
Henry Cattan

Illustrations by Christian Buléon

Saqi Books

To Eva

British Library Cataloguing-in-Publication Data
A catalogue record for this book is available from the
British Library

ISBN 0 86356 958 7 (hb)
ISBN 0 86356 354 6 (pb)

© Louis Cattan, 2000

First published in hardback by Namara Publications Ltd, 1979

This edition first published 2000

Saqi Books
26 Westbourne Grove
London W2 5RH

Contents

Acknowledgements

The author is indebted to the following publishers for permission to reproduce some of the anecdotes appearing in this book: John Murray (Publishers) Ltd, for the three anecdotes from *Persian Proverbs* by L. P. Elwell-Sutton; Routledge and Kegan Paul Ltd and the Regents of the University of California, for a citation from *The Life and Works of Jahiz* by Charles Pellat; Luzac and Co., for seven anecdotes from *Laughable Stories of Bar-Hebraeus*, translated from the Syriac by E. A. W. Budge, 1897; M. Siavash-Danesh and Vahid Publishing Co., Teheran, for four anecdotes derived from *An Anthology of Persian Prose*; and Editions G. P. Maisonneuve et Larose, for one anecdote from *Contes Arabes*, by R. Basset, Paris, 1924.

In all cases the source of the anecdote is mentioned in the endnotes to Part I.

Foreword

Henry Cattan collected in this book some of the best anecdotes, tales, stories and proverbs found in Arabic literature.

The most universally famous works of Arabic literature are the *Thousand and One Nights* and *Kalilah and Dimnah*. The tales of the *Thousand and One Nights* are of Persian origin and were translated into Arabic during the ninth century. Arab storytellers have added to them, drawing on Arab and Greek sources. Many of the characters featured in these tales are imaginary creatures and jinns who, according to popular belief, can be either malevolent or benevolent. They all inhabit a world of extraordinary adventure where magic blends with the familiar, and wisdom with absurdity.

Kalilah and Dimnah contains stories of animals that talk and behave as humans, stories that are lessons in morality and statecraft. These tales were translated from Persian by Ibn Al Muqaffa' (734–757). The behaviour of the king of the animals caused offence to caliph al-Mansour, who suspected that it alluded to him, and the translator was sentenced to death. The importance of *Kalilah and Dimnah* resides above all in the simplicity of its style and the sheer quality of its storytelling, features which have influenced a good many Arab authors.

In addition to these two seminal works, there are a considerable number of stories, tales and anecdotes in other genres: literary, theological and anecdotal. The author of this collection has selected some examples whose interest and charm will not be lost in translation. Most of them are of Arab origin, some from Indo-Persian sources, and others inspired by Aesop's celebrated fables.

The chief consideration governing the choice of stories for this book was that they should offer a human interest or reflect Oriental wit and humour. Fairy-tales and stories about jinns and supernatural beings which tend to dominate oriental folklore were not included. Other stories, whose flavour would otherwise be lost by too slavish a rendering of the original text, have been adapted by the author. Few of the anecdotes collected in this work have previously been translated. Where they have appeared before, in English or French, this has been acknowledged in an explanatory footnote. All those selected in this way are contained in the first part of this book.

The second part is a selection of what are called the Juha stories. These stories, which number several hundred, constitute the mainstay of Arab popular humour and are widespread all over the Middle East. The Juha stories possess a distinctive combination of humorous simplicity and a kind of illogical logic. Their hero Juha, named Goha in Egypt, has been claimed as their own by both Arabs and Turks.

From the eighth century onwards, Arab writers allude to a man called Juha or Abu Ghosn, living in Kufa in Iraq, with a reputation for being naive and comic. His counterpart in Turkey is of more recent date. He is called Khoja Nasreddin al-Roumi and is thought to have lived in Turkey during the thirteenth century. In Iran the same guileless figure bears the name of Mullah Nasreddin. Whether Juha really existed or not, the Juha stories may be considered as the fruit of the popular imagination of the Middle East.

The third part of this anthology contains a selection of Arabic proverbs, some philosophical some just witty. The Arabs possess more than seven thousand proverbs, maxims and popular sayings relating to all aspects of life and reflecting human experience. Many are still frequently used to ornament a conversation or emphasize an argument. As human wisdom is universal, the reader should not be surprised to find many that have a familiar ring to them. They may sometimes be expressed differently but their meaning will often be almost identical to proverbs told in other languages.

My late father collected the themes of this work for his own pleasure and translated them for the benefit of western readers. It is rewarding that a new generation of readers will be able to enjoy the wit and wisdom of the contents.

Louis H. Cattan, 1999

PART I

ANECDOTES AND FABLES FROM ARAB AND PERSIAN LITERATURE

THE DEVIL AND THE VINE

After Adam planted the vine, the Devil (may God curse him) brought a peacock, killed it and poured its blood over the bed of the plant. Later, when the buds of the vine appeared, the Devil slew a monkey over it and the plant soaked up its blood. Again, when the vine bore fruit, the Devil slaughtered over it a lion and the plant drew up its blood. Then when it bore no more fruit, the Devil killed a pig and sprinkled the animal's blood over the vine's stalk.

As a result of this, we observe the drinker of wine is at first seized with vanity and admiration for himself, like a peacock. Then, as he becomes slightly more drunk, he starts to jump, caper and gesticulate like a monkey. As he continues to drink, he turns into a lion, becomes quarrelsome and spoils for a fight. In the end, when he has drunk his fill, he stumbles around, falls down and sleeps like a pig.[1]

AL-HAJJAJ AND THE BEDOUIN

Al-Hajjaj, the emir of Iraq,[2] was well known for his excessive severity, and was greatly feared by his people.

One day he went out hunting in the desert. At a certain moment, he outdistanced his guards and encountered a bedouin who knew nothing about his identity or rank. It occurred to the emir that this would be a good occasion for him to learn at first hand what the people thought of their masters. He stopped the bedouin and asked him where he was from and what he thought of the king's representatives. The bedouin replied that they were the worst of all people, unjust, cruel and corrupt. The emir then asked him, 'What do you think of al-Hajjaj, the emir of Iraq?'

The bedouin replied, 'Iraq never had any ruler worse than he, may God curse his soul and whoever appointed him to rule over this country!'

At these words al-Hajjaj shook with anger and shouted at the bedouin, 'Do you know who I am? I am al-Hajjaj!' Completely unruffled, the bedouin asked al-Hajjaj, 'Do you know who I am? I am the fool of Beni Ijel tribe! From time to time I suffer from fits and today I am subject to one of them!'

Al-Hajjaj laughed and let him go.[3]

A TASTE OF INJUSTICE

When he was a boy and heir to the throne of Persia, Chosroës I[4] was placed in the hands of a tutor who was entrusted with his instruction and education. Chosroës proved to be a very good and disciplined pupil, but one day his tutor beat him, without good reason or fault on his part. From that day the boy harboured in his heart a deep rancour against his tutor.

When Chosroës grew up and ascended the throne in succession to his father, one of his first acts was to send for his former tutor and ask him why he had beaten him unjustly and without reason. His teacher replied, 'Sire, I knew you would one day ascend the throne and rule over many peoples and territories in a vast empire. I therefore wanted you to learn the taste of injustice so that you should not be unjust to others.'[5]

THE PROOF OF THE DEPOSIT

Being about to depart on pilgrimage to Mecca, a man left his money in safekeeping with a neighbour. Upon his return he went to the neighbour and asked for his money back, but the neighbour denied any knowledge of the transaction. Thereupon, the man took his neighbour to Iyass, a judge famed for his perspicacity, and submitted to him his complaint. The judge asked him about the place where, in accordance with his claim, he handed the money to his neighbour. The plaintiff replied that he had handed over the money under a large carob tree at a certain place outside the city which he described. The judge then asked the plaintiff whether any witnesses were present when he gave the money to his neighbour. The plaintiff replied, 'God is my witness.'

Questioned by the judge, the defendant denied ever having received any money for safekeeping from the plaintiff. He also denied knowledge of the carob tree mentioned by the plaintiff.

Thereupon, the judge ordered the plaintiff to go to the place where he alleged the transaction had taken place in the hope that by looking at the carob tree either he might find a sign that would help him to prove his claim, or he might perhaps remember he had buried the money somewhere near the tree.

The plaintiff did as he was ordered by the judge, and hurried to the place which he had described. Meanwhile the judge ordered the defendant to sit in a corner of the courtroom to await his opponent's return. The judge himself then proceeded with the hearing of other cases.

Some time later, the judge turned to the defendant and abruptly asked him, 'Do you think your opponent has had time to reach the carob tree?' Taken unawares, the defendant replied, 'No, my lord, he cannot have reached the carob tree yet.'

This reply showed that the defendant had lied in denying knowledge of the carob tree under which the deposit had taken place. Being thus furnished with convincing proof in support of the plaintiff's claim from the defendant's own mouth, the judge ordered that the defendant be taken into custody. At this point the defendant broke down and admitted the truth of the plaintiff's story and undertook to pay back to him the debt in full.

Accordingly, upon the plaintiff's return, the judge told him that during his absence the defendant had admitted his claim, and he gave judgment in his favour.[6]

AN OATH TO THE THIEVES

One night thieves broke into a house. After gagging the owner, they took all articles of value they could find. Before they left, fearing that the owner might have recognized them and would reveal their identity to the police, they thought of killing him. Their leader, however, suggested that the householder's life should be spared if he agreed to take an oath on the Qur'an not to open his mouth to disclose their identity. The householder swore an oath to that effect and was thus saved from certain death.

On the following day, the victim saw his furniture and possessions being sold openly by the thieves in the souq and it grieved him that he could not open his mouth in protest on account of his oath. So he went to Abu Hanifa[7] and consulted him about what to do.

After hearing the man's story, Abu Hanifa sent for the elders of the quarter where the man lived and instructed them to act in the following way. First, they should gather in the mosque all the people of their quarter who were known to be of ill repute. When all the suspects should be assembled, the victim of the theft would take position at the door of the mosque, and the suspects would then be released from the mosque one by one. As each one came to the door, the victim of the theft would be asked, 'Is this man one of the thieves?' If the man shown to him were not one of the thieves, he would speak and say no. If, however, the man should be, in fact, one of the thieves, he would keep silent and would not open his mouth.

The elders did as they had been instructed by Abu Hanifa. In this manner the thieves were identified and arrested one by one, without the victim having uttered a single word in violation of his oath.[8]

FITTING THE CRIME TO THE PUNISHMENT

A slave was engaged in the service of a king. On the first day of his entry into the royal service, there was a state dinner at the king's palace and the slave was ordered to assist in serving at the king's table. He was handed a large plate which contained mutton, vegetables and sauce, and was asked to lay it before the king and his guests.

On approaching His Majesty's august presence and seeing for the first time the king in all his glory, the slave was suddenly seized with awe and fear. His hands trembled and a few drops of the sauce fell from the plate upon the king's embroidered garments. Greatly angered, the king's immediate reaction was to order the servant to be taken away and beheaded. On hearing that this punishment was to be meted out to him, the slave was convinced that whatever he might now do could not expose him to any greater misfortune, and he emptied

upon the king's head and on his beautiful garments the contents of the plate – meat, vegetables and sauce.

Thereupon the guards rushed at the culprit and seized him. The king, boiling with rage, shouted at him, 'Woe to you! Why have you done this?'

The slave replied, 'Sire, what I have done was meant only to protect your name and to safeguard your reputation. I was afraid that the people would despise you and think you a tyrant for having put me to death for a slight offence which was done without malice or intent. I have, therefore, perpetrated this greater crime so that its enormity would justify the punishment you are about to inflict on me.'

Upon hearing these words, the king realized that he was about to commit a very grave injustice. He stifled his anger, and turning to the slave said to him, 'Your good excuse redeems the evil of your deed. You are pardoned for what you have done.' And he rewarded him by granting him his freedom.[9]

THE CHILD HE LOVED BEST

A man was asked which of his children he loved best. He replied, 'The youngest until he grows up, the sick one until he recovers, and the absent one until he returns.'[10]

A RARE *SAVOIR-FAIRE*

A lion, a wolf and a fox went out hunting together, and they killed a wild ass, a gazelle and a rabbit. The lion asked the wolf to divide the quarry among them. The wolf said without hesitation, 'The wild ass goes to you, the gazelle to me, and the rabbit to our friend the fox.' Infuriated by the wolf's proposed division, the lion struck him violently with his paw and severed his head from his body.

The lion then turned to the fox and said to him, 'Now you divide between us.' The fox bowed to the lion with great deference and said in a meek voice, 'Your Majesty, the division is quite simple. The wild ass will be your lunch, and the gazelle will be for your dinner. As for the rabbit, it will serve as a titbit for you between meals.'

The lion said to him, 'What tact, what taste and what rare savoir-faire! How well cognizant you are of the proper rules! What I should like to know is who taught you how to make such an admirable division?'

'The wolf's head lying over there!' came the fox's reply.[11]

THE DIVISION OF THE CHICKENS

A man from Basra told the following story:

A bedouin came from the desert and I offered him hospitality at my house. I had a wife, two sons and two daughters. I had also many chickens. So I said to my wife, 'Go and roast a chicken for our lunch.'

When lunch was brought, we all sat down, I, my wife, my sons and daughters and the bedouin. Meaning to make fun of our guest, by asking him to perform what I thought would be a most difficult job, I pushed the chicken towards him and asked him to divide it amongst us. 'I am not very good at dividing chickens,' he said, 'but if you accept my division, I shall divide it among you.'

We insisted that he should do so. Thereupon, he cut off the head of the chicken and gave it to me saying, 'The head is for the head of the house.' He then cut off the two wings and said, 'The two wings are for the two boys.' Next he cut off the two legs and said, 'The two legs are for the two girls.' Finally he cut off the parson's nose, passed it to my wife and said, 'The parson's nose is for the old woman and the breast is for the guest.' He thus got the best part of the chicken and the joke turned out to be at our expense.

In the evening I asked my wife to roast for us five chickens for dinner. When we sat down to eat, I asked the bedouin to divide the chickens amongst us. The bedouin said, 'I have an idea that you were not happy at the way I divided the chicken for lunch.'

We protested that we had no such thought and insisted that he should divide the chickens amongst us. The bedouin inquired, 'Do you want the division in even or in odd numbers?'

We replied, 'In odd numbers.'

Thereupon, he seized one chicken, passed it to me and said, 'You, your wife and one fowl make three.' He then passed one chicken to my two sons and said, 'You two boys and a fowl make three.' He did the same thing with the two girls. Finally, he took the two remaining chickens for himself, saying, 'I and two fowls make three.' The joke was again at our expense.

Seeing us eye in amazement the two chickens in his hands, the bedouin said, 'Perhaps you don't like the division in odd numbers? But this is the only way it can be done. Maybe you would rather have a division in even numbers?'

In the hope of getting a better deal, we gratefully answered in unison that we would prefer a division in even numbers. So he took all the chickens back and placed them in front of him. 'You, your two sons and one fowl,' he said, make four,' and he passed me one chicken. 'The old woman, her two daughters and one fowl make four,' he said and passed to my wife and my two daughters one chicken. 'I and three chickens make four,' he said, and he took for himself the three remaining chickens. He then lifted his hands to heaven and exclaimed, 'Praise be to Thee, O God, for Thou hast inspired me!'[12]

THE CALIPH'S REWARD

Haroun al-Rashid[13] had spent a long sleepless night and his servants found him in the morning gloomy, dejected and bad tempered. His trusted servant Masrour said to him that he knew a popular jester called Ibn al-Ghazali who made people roar with laughter at his jokes, and he suggested that he should bring him to the palace in the hope that his humorous anecdotes would amuse the caliph and restore to him his sense of gaiety and his usual good humour. The caliph ordered him to bring Ibn al-Ghazali to the palace without delay.

Masrour hurried out in the streets of Baghdad to the jester's house and asked him to accompany him to the palace to amuse the caliph. Masrour, however, insisted upon one condition: the jester must agree to share with him the reward which the caliph usually gave to the jester on such occasions. Ibn al-Ghazali agreed to share with Masrour the anticipated reward, but the two men disagreed on the manner of its division. The jester proposed that the reward should be divided equally between them, but Masrour insisted on receiving two-thirds of it. The jester argued and reasoned with him but without avail. Eventually, Ibn al-Ghazali gave in and accepted with reluctance to cede to Masrour two-thirds of the reward.

Masrour then led the jester to the royal palace and introduced him

into the caliph's presence. The jester told the caliph his best jokes and related to him his most amusing anecdotes, but he could not cheer him up or draw even a faint smile from him. The caliph remained sour and sullen.

Despite his lack of success, the jester continued his babble and chatter but this merely irritated the caliph. Suddenly the caliph shouted at him, 'I am sick and tired of your vulgar jokes and your silly stories!' Then turning to the chief of his guards, he ordered him to administer to the jester then and there three strokes of his whip, and send him away.

The guards seized the jester and their chief proceeded to carry out the caliph's order. After the first stroke, the jester shouted, 'Stop! Stop for God's sake! I have something to say. Then, turning to the caliph he said, 'Pardon me, Sire, if you wish justice to be done, your servant Masrour should get the two remaining strokes.'

Intrigued by the jester's request, the caliph asked him to explain. Ibn al-Ghazali told the caliph about the deal Masrour had made with him regarding the sharing of the reward. In accordance with the arrangement, two of the strokes, he claimed, should be administered to Masrour. On hearing this story, Haroun al-Rashid burst into long and loud laughter. He then turned to Masrour and asked him, 'Do you still want your share of the reward?'

'No, Sire,' replied Masrour, 'I donate my share to Ibn al-Ghazali!' The caliph again laughed and ordered his treasurer to give to the jester a reward before sending him away.[14]

THE GRAMMARIAN AND THE SAILOR

A man learned in the science of grammar undertook a sea voyage.

During the voyage he asked the sailor, 'Do you know anything of the science of grammar?'

The sailor replied that he did not.

'Then,' commented the grammarian, 'you have lost one half of your life!'

Later, during the voyage, a violent storm broke out, winds and waves swept and tossed the vessel like a feather, and the small boat was about to sink. The sailor asked the grammarian, 'Do you know how to swim?'

The grammarian said that he did not.

Thereupon the sailor said to him, 'Then, you have lost the whole of your life!'

CATCHING WILD DUCKS

Al-Jahez[15] has described a novel way to catch ducks which was in use in Iraq during his lifetime. Al-Jahez says:

I asked one of those who were known to catch one hundred ducks in a day how he performed this feat. He had about this number in front of him and he said, 'What you see here is not the catch of one day, but the catch of one hour. This is how we do it. We go to a marsh where wild ducks assemble in great numbers. We float a large dry pumpkin on the surface of the water so that the wind takes them towards the birds. At first, they are somewhat frightened at the sight of the pumpkin bouncing up and down on top of the water and floating towards them. But it does not take long for them to get accustomed to the sight of the pumpkin, and their alarm soon subsides.

'As soon as we are certain that the ducks are no longer alarmed by

the sight of the pumpkin, one of us caps his head with a pumpkin, the neck of which has previously been cut off large enough to allow a man's head to go into it. Two holes are made in the pumpkin level with the eyes, so that the hunter can see through them. The hunter then wades slowly through the water towards the ducks, his head only covered by the pumpkin moving towards them. Coming close to the birds, the hunter stretches his hand under the water, seizes one duck by its legs, pulls it down below the surface, snaps off its wings and then leaves it afloat. The duck cannot fly away but continues to swim or float, thus causing no suspicion among the other birds. By this means, the hunter is able to catch, one after another, all the ducks in the marsh.'[16]

THE ASTROLOGER'S MISFORTUNE

An astrologer invited some of his friends to come to his home one evening so that he might show them the stars, and explain their movements, their qualities, and their influence on the universe. His friends came, and after nightfall he led them to his garden where he began to walk around, pointing out the stars, explaining their names and describing how, from their study and observation, astrologers are able to see through the obscurity of the future and perceive their influence on the affairs of men and the events of the world. While in the midst of his discourse, the astrologer, who was leading the party through the shadows of the garden, suddenly fell into a well. As he was being pulled out of the well, he observed, 'This is the misfortune of astrologers: they know what is above them, but are quite unaware of what is below them.'[17]

THE MAN DESERVED HIS PUNISHMENT!

A story told by Obeid Zakani, a Persian writer:

A man claimed that he was God. He was led to the caliph to be tried and punished for his abominable crime. The caliph said to him, 'Last year a man claimed he was a prophet and he was hanged. What dost thou say to that?' The man answered, 'Thou didst well to have him hanged for I did not send him!'[18]

DO YOU KNOW WHO I AM?

While on a hunting expedition, al-Mahdi,[19] Commander of the Faithful, lost his way in the desert and was separated from his suite. He came upon a bedouin who was eating. In accordance with custom, the bedouin invited al-Mahdi to partake of his food. Being hungry and thirsty, al-Mahdi accepted the invitation. The bedouin gave him food and poured for him a cup of wine from a goatskin. Having emptied his cup, al-Mahdi asked the man, 'Do you know who I am?'

'No,' came the reply.

'I am a friend of the grand vizier and I shall put in a good word for you with him which will benefit you.'

The bedouin thanked him and poured for him a second cup of wine. Al-Mahdi drank the second cup and then asked the man, 'Do you know who I am?'

'Didn't you tell me that you were a friend of the grand vizier?' asked the bedouin.

'I am the Grand Vizier,' said al-Mahdi.

The bedouin said, 'God bless you and prolong your life.'

A little later, after drinking a third cup, al-Mahdi turned to the bedouin and exclaimed, 'Do you know who I am?'

'Just say who you are and let me judge,' replied the bedouin cautiously.

'I am the Commander of the Faithful in person,' said al-Mahdi.

On hearing these words, the bedouin quickly pulled the wine goatskin away and put it out of the reach of his guest. Al-Mahdi noticed his response and remarked to him,, 'Why did you hurry to put the wine away?'

'Well,' replied the man, 'after drinking three cups you have claimed to be the caliph. By God, were you to drink a fourth cup, I fear that you will claim to be the Prophet!'[20]

AN UNWISE COUNSEL

Khaled Ibn Safwan[21] said:

Once I paid a visit to al-Saffah[22] and found him alone, I said to him, 'O Commander of the Faithful, I pray you to order that the screen (which separates the caliph's room from the women's quarters) be drawn so that I may offer you some valuable counsel which will be of advantage you.' The caliph ordered that the screen be drawn so that we could not be seen from the women's quarters.

'O Commander of the Faithful', I said to him, 'I have pondered over your situation and over what God has placed in your hands and I have come to the conclusion that of all people you are the most harassed and deprived of the pleasures of life.

'How is this?', asked the caliph with interest and surprise.

'This is because you have restricted yourself to one wife only, and have forsaken the beautiful white virgins', I replied.

'O Khaled', said the caliph, 'I have not heard this kind of speech before.'

I then requested the caliph's leave to withdraw and went away.

A short time later Umm Salameh (the caliph's wife) came and found the caliph worried and depressed. 'O Commander of the Faithful', she asked, 'I see you worried and thoughtful. What is the matter? Have you heard any news that has saddened you?'

'I have not been disturbed by any bad news', replied the caliph, 'but by what Khaled Ibn Safwan told me just now', and he ingenuously repeated to her what Khaled had said to him.

'And what did you say to this son of a whore?' Umm Salameh asked. 'He counsels me and you speak ill of him?' exclaimed the caliph with pain and surprise.

Umm Salameh left the caliph and immediately called some of her trusted servants who she knew were devoted to her. 'It is for a day like this', she told them, 'that I have taken you into my service. Go out and look for Khaled Ibn Safwan and when you find him beat him until you break all his bones!'

Khaled Ibn Safwan pursued his story:

Umm Salameh's men searched for me everywhere but I hid from them.

At the same time the caliph, apparently wanting to learn more about the subject which I had discussed with him, also asked his men to look for me. So one day I was discovered by the caliph's men and they took me, quite terrified, to a palace. When I was brought into the caliph's presence, I heard a muttering sound behind the screen and I thought, 'By God, it must be Umm Salameh.'

The caliph asked me, 'Where have you been all this time?'

'I was attending to some of my crops', I replied.

'I want you to repeat to me and enlarge upon what you told me some time ago about the beautiful white virgins', said the caliph.

'Oh yes, O Commander of the Faithful', I said. 'The Arabs have always considered that if a husband takes a second wife, he commits a terrible mistake because a second wife is a source of mischief. A man who has two wives is between two fires, one of which consumes him with its heat, while the other burns him with its flame.'

'This is not what you told me!' exclaimed the caliph.

'Yes', I insisted. 'And I told you also that four wives are the source of worry, pain, anguish and quarrel.'[23]

'This is not at all what I heard from you!' shouted the caliph.

'Indeed it is,' I said, 'and I told you also that Umm Salameh was the most beautiful flower in your garden and when you expressed a desire to marry again I protested that this was not a sensible thing to do at your age!'

'You are a liar!' shouted the caliph.

'I have to choose the lesser of two evils and I don't have much choice between telling a lie and having my bones broken by the men of Umm Salameh!' I whispered in the ear of the caliph.

At that moment laughing was heard behind the screen and the caliph realized with amusement the reason for the change in my language and counsel to him.

The caliph let me go and when I returned home that day I found that valuable presents had been delivered there for me by the servants of Umm Salameh.[24]

THE NEIGHBOURHOOD OF THE POET

A man who was a neighbour of Abou Doulaf,[25] a poet of Baghdad, fell into debt and decided to sell his house in order to pay off his creditors. He asked one thousand dinars for it. People said to him: 'But your house is not worth more than five hundred dinars. How can you expect to sell it at one thousand?'

'True,' the man replied, 'I sell the house for only five hundred dinars, and I sell the neighbourhood of Abou Doulaf for another five hundred dinars.'

When this remark reached the ears of Abou Doulaf, he was so moved that he paid off the man's debts and told him, 'I don't wish to lose you as my neighbour!'[26]

THE CAMEL AND ITS LOAD OF SALT

A man owned a camel and earned his living by using it to carry sacks of salt from a quarry to the town. As he was paid in proportion to the number of sacks he transported, he decided to increase his earnings by increasing the load of his camel. However, the overloading greatly exhausted the camel, who lost weight and energy.

One day the camel complained of his misfortune to another camel, who was older and wiser, and asked for his advice. The wise old camel said to him, 'The remedy is easy. When you cross the river on your way to town, do not allow your load to remain above the water, but stoop down in the river. The salt will dissolve and this will lighten your load.'

The camel followed the counsel given to him, and on his next trip, when he reached the river, he crouched down in the water. His owner tried to make him stand up, shouted and shrieked, beat and kicked him, but without avail. The camel remained in the water until almost half his load was dissolved. When he rose, he felt little weight on his back. Having found that the trick worked, the camel repeated his trick on other trips until his owner was forced to abandon his business of transporting salt, and thus lost his only means of livelihood.

Then one day the owner of the camel was hired to carry sacks of wool to the town. He loaded his camel with the sacks and when he reached the river the camel resorted to the same stratagem: he dipped into the water with his load. But contrary to his expectations this device did not lighten his load. Indeed, the wool absorbed the water and the load became much heavier; so much heavier, in fact, that the camel could not rise and was almost drowned. At the risk of his life, the camel learned his lesson: a good trick does not always work twice.[27]

THE MAN WHO DID NOT WANT TO LIVE NEAR A MOSQUE

A man came to live in a new town and sent his servant in search of a house. He asked his servant to find him a house which should not be close to a mosque because, as he explained to him, he preferred amusement to prayer.

The servant went in search of a suitable house and eventually rented one which was located between two mosques. The master flew into a rage.

'Didn't I tell you to find me a house which was not too close to a mosque?' he yelled at his servant.

'You don't understand the reason for my choice, master,' said the servant. 'The house which I have rented for you answers your purpose beautifully. The people who attend the first mosque will think that you have gone to prayers at the other mosque, while the people of the other mosque will assume that you are praying at the first mosque!'[28]

THE SNAKE CHARMER AND THE MOUSE

A snake charmer[29] was asked by a man one day to come to his house to kill a big snake which hid there and terrified the owner and his family. The snake charmer came and found the snake's hole. He began to chant his incantations and after a little while the snake stuck its head out of the hole. With a firm and unhesitating hand the snake charmer seized the snake by the back of the neck and pulled it out of the hole. As he was about to whirl it around in the air by its tail and kill it by striking it violently against the ground he saw the snake vomit a small mouse it had swallowed. The snake charmer happened to be one of those people who are terrified by the sight of a mouse. When he saw the mouse he was so scared that he threw down the snake and ran away as fast as he could. The people were not a little amazed to find in this snake charmer the extraordinary combination of a rare courage and an absurd fear.[30]

THE MONKS AND THE PRECIOUS STONE

Two travelling monks who lived in prayer and from charity after a long journey reached Al Ahwaz, a town in Persia. One of them went to beg for food while the other sat down to rest near a jeweller's shop. While he sat there, a well-dressed woman emerged from one of the neighbouring palaces carrying a jewel–box full of precious stones. As she came near the jeweller's shop, her foot slipped and the jewel–box broke open and the precious stones were scattered everywhere. The largest and most valuable of the stones fell near an ostrich which belonged to a neighbour and which happened to be nearby. The ostrich, dazzled by the glittering stone, instantly swallowed it. Only the monk had seen what the ostrich had done.

At the cries of the woman, the jeweller and his apprentices rushed out from their shop and helped her to gather the precious stones, but the woman immediately noticed the disappearance of the largest and most valuable one. She began screaming, and a crowd collected. As the monk was the only person in the vicinity at the time of the incident, suspicion fell on him. He was asked about the precious stone, but he denied taking it. He felt reluctant to disclose that the ostrich had swallowed the stone for fear that it would be killed and that he would be responsible for shedding its blood. The people, however, did not believe him and they searched him and beat him severely. When his companion returned he was also suspected of having taken away the stone to hide it, so he too was severely beaten.

At this point, a wise old man happened to pass by and asked why the two monks were being beaten. Having been told what had happened, he looked round carefully and saw the ostrich nearby. He asked the people, 'Was this ostrich around when the precious stones fell to the ground?' The people replied in the affirmative. The old man then said, 'The ostrich must be the culprit.' Thereupon, the value of the ostrich was paid to its owner, and it was killed and its belly opened. The old man was right: the precious stone was found in the stomach of the ostrich.[31]

DUEL BY POISON

A certain king was haunted by the fear of being poisoned by his enemies. He, therefore, ordered a search to be made in his kingdom for the doctor most adept at combating the effects of poison so that the man might be engaged in his service and attached to his person.

The search led to the discovery of two famous doctors who were rivals. But there still remained the problem of deciding who was the better doctor of the two. This problem was resolved by the grand vizier, who suggested that the issue be settled by a duel between the two rival candidates. The duel would be by poison: each of the two doctors would take a poison offered to him by the other and then combat it by an antidote which he would have prepared in advance. The winner would win the envied post of king's physician. The two rivals accepted this form of duel.

A day was fixed for the duel, which was held in the presence of the king and his ministers. Lots were drawn to determine which of the two opponents should be the first to tender the poison to his rival. The doctor who won the draw had concocted a poisonous beverage which was so terrible that it would have dissolved a black stone. He presented to his rival a cup containing the beverage, and the latter drank it to the last drop. Immediately afterwards, he swallowed an antidote which rendered him completely immune to the poison.

When his turn came to administer a poisonous substance to his rival, he said that he would not give him any liquid to drink, or any substance to eat, but only something to smell. Thereupon he produced a rose, breathed on it and, after reciting an incantation, passed it to his rival and invited him to smell it. The rival took the rose with a trembling hand, smelt it and dropped dead on the spot.

The king then asked the winner of the duel to explain what kind of poison he had put in the rose. The winner explained that the rose contained no poison and was absolutely harmless; his rival had died, not from any poison or magic, but simply out of fear.[32]

THE TRAVELLER WITH THE POOR APPETITE

A traveller came upon a hermit who lived alone in a mountain cave near Jericho and asked him if he had anything to give him to eat. The hermit invited the visitor to sit down, and brought a loaf of bread which he placed in front of him. He then went to fetch a plate of lentil soup. On his return he was amazed to find that his visitor had already eaten the loaf of bread. So he placed the plate of soup in front of him and went to fetch some more bread. Returning with another loaf, he discovered that the visitor had already devoured the soup. This business went on for a while, the hermit rushing to and fro, no sooner bringing the bread than the soup had gone, and no sooner getting more soup than the bread was eaten up.

The hermit paused and asked the visitor the object of his journey. The visitor explained that he was on his way to a famous doctor in Damascus whose treatment he sought because his appetite was poor. On his way back, he added, he would stop and pay him his respects.

Alarmed by the traveller's future plans, especially should the famous doctor of Damascus succeed in improving his appetite further, the hermit told his visitor not to try to see him on his way back, as on the morrow he would be leaving on a pilgrimage and would be away for a long, long time. 'In any case,' he added, 'I bid you goodbye in advance!'[33]

THE THREE THIEVES AND THE BOX OF JEWELS

Three thieves stole a box of jewels and hid themselves to divide their loot. As the division of the loot was likely to take some time and they were hungry, they decided to eat first. Accordingly, they despatched one of their number to the market to buy some food.

On his way to the market the thief thought to himself, 'Why don't I poison the food which I shall take back with me and thus get rid of my two companions: in this way I shall keep the jewels to myself alone.' In furtherance of his scheme, he bought some rat poison which he mixed with the food he brought back to his companions.

Meanwhile, his two companions concocted a plan of their own: they plotted that on his return they would kill him, and have the jewels for themselves.

So when the third man returned with the food, his two companions sprang on him and murdered him. They then sat down, and ate their last meal.[34]

AN AMENDED PRESCRIPTION

When a certain man came to a physician to consult him about an attack of colic, the physician said to him, 'Eat a few thorns.' The man then brought out ink and paper to write upon, and said to the physician, 'What dost thou advise?'

The physician said to him, 'Eat a few thorns, together with a bushel of barley.'

And the man said, 'Thou saidst nothing at all about barley at first,' and the physician replied to him, 'No, I did not, for I did not know until this moment that thou wert an ass.'[35]

THE MAN WHO OWNED THE BRIDLE

One of the spectators at a horse race was so overjoyed when the black horse won that he started shouting, jumping and applauding with great excitement. Intrigued, the people around asked him, 'Are you the owner of the winning horse?'

'No,' he shouted back, 'but I own its bridle!'[36]

THE SHEIKH'S TEARS

An old sheikh set a trap to catch birds and took up position to watch not far away. Each time a bird was caught in the trap, he would hurry to wring its neck and push it into a bag. The weather was bitterly cold and as he went about his business tears came to his eyes.

The birds became alarmed at the disappearance of many of their companions, and they met together to discuss the situation. When some of them expressed suspicion of the old sheikh and his doings, others protested and said, 'This sheikh is a venerable and compassionate-looking old man as one can see from the tears that run down from his eyes.'

But one of the birds who was wiser than the others observed, 'Do not look at the tears running down from his eyes, but at what his hands are doing.'[37]

THIS I CAN EASILY DO!

During the reign of al-Ma'moun[38] a man was brought before him accused of the grave offence of claiming to be a prophet.

Al-Ma'moun said to the accused, 'Prophets have signs, they perform miracles. If a prophet is thrown into the fire, he will come out of it unscathed. To test you, we shall light a fire, throw you into it, and

if you come out of it unharmed, we shall accept your claim to be a prophet.'

The accused said he would prefer a simpler test.

Al-Ma'moun then said to him: 'Take Moses. Look at what he did. He threw his rod before the Pharaoh and it became a serpent. He stretched out his hand over the sea and the sea drew back.'

The man said: 'This is even harder than being thrown into the fire. I want something less difficult as a test.'

Al-Ma'moun then said, 'Take the proofs given by Christ.'

'What were the proofs given by Christ?' inquired the accused.

'Christ restored the dead to life,' observed al-Ma'moun.

'Oh, this I can easily do!' said the accused. 'Have your grand vizier who is standing there beside you beheaded and I undertake to bring him immediately back to life.'

The grand vizier who had no wish to lend himself to such a demonstration said to the accused: 'I am the first to believe that you are a genuine prophet!'[39]

THE QUALITIES HE REQUIRED OF THE DONKEY

A Sheikh wanted to buy a donkey which he could ride on his errands. He went to the market and told the broker, 'I want you to find me a donkey who is neither too small, nor too big; if the road is clear, he will hurry but, if it is crowded, he will slow his pace; if well fed, he will be thankful but, if underfed, he will be content; and who, if I ride him, will fly like the wind, but if another rides him, will drag his feet.'

The broker told the sheikh, 'Such a remarkable animal cannot easily be found. I would, however, advise you to be patient. If God will metamorphose our chief justice, Sheikh Ibn Abi Laylah,[40] and change him into a donkey, I shall buy him for you.'[41]

THE CRANE'S REWARD

A small bone stuck in the throat of a wolf. It caused him great pain and he could not get it out. In despair, he went to a crane, and asked him to pull out the bone from his throat with his beak, promising him a reward for his service. The crane put his beak into the wolf's mouth, and pulled out the bone. As the wolf turned to go away the crane asked him for his reward, but the wolf replied, 'Isn't it a sufficient satisfaction for you that you succeeded in performing the rare exploit of taking your head safely out of my mouth? And yet you dare to ask for a reward in addition?'[42]

MY DONKEY NEVER HAD A TAIL

A debtor was being dragged by his creditor to the qadi of Balkh, a city in Afghanistan. Hoping to escape, he dashed through the open door of a house and up the stairs on to the roof. Unfortunately for him, there was no other way down, and in jumping into the neighbouring yard he landed on the neighbour's wife, who was pregnant. As a result she had a miscarriage. The infuriated husband seized upon the debtor, who, seeing that 'when the water has covered his head, a hundred fathoms are as one', told him to join the creditor and see the qadi.

A little further along the road a runaway horse was being chased. The debtor, trying to be helpful, threw a stone at it, and the stone hit the horse in the eye, blinding it. The owner came up in a rage, and the debtor told him, 'We are all on our way to the qadi; you had better come with us.'

They came next to an overloaded ass that had fallen down in the

mud, and its owner asked the four men for help. They all took hold of it, the debtor grasping the tail; and as luck would have it, when he pulled, the tail came right off. The owner began to abuse the debtor, but the latter said to him, 'All right, you too had better come to the qadi.'

Finally they came to the qadi's house, and as they went in, the debtor secretly concealed a large stone under his coat. As he bowed to the qadi, he surreptitiously pointed to the bulge in his coat, implying that it was a purse of gold. The qadi took the hint, and then called on the creditor to state his case. The debtor flatly denied his claim, and since the creditor had no papers in support of them, the qadi sent him away empty-handed.

Then the husband came forward and told his story. The qadi replied, 'Very well, this woman must go and stay in the defendant's house until she is once more pregnant; he must be liable for all her expenses, and during this period her husband must not come near her.' The husband protested violently against this decision, and finally the qadi ruled that, in consideration of the payment of five hundred rials by the husband to the debtor, all claims and counter-claims between them should be cancelled.

Next the horse-owner came forward, and the qadi said, 'Certainly the defendant must pay damages, but in order that we may assess them fairly, the horse is to be sawn in half, and the half with the sound eye sold in the bazaar; whatever price it fetches will be a fair valuation of the half that the defendant has damaged.' The owner protested violently and finally it was decided that the debtor should receive a sum of one hundred rials from the horse-owner and should keep the horse.

Meanwhile the owner of the donkey had been watching all this

with growing concern, and when his turn came, he tried to sneak out of the court. The qadi called after him, 'Where are you going, my friend? Come and state your case.'

But the donkey's owner replied, 'I have no complaint, your honour; I swear that my donkey never had a tail, even as a colt!'[43]

THE MOST BEAUTIFUL DREAM

A Muslim, a Christian and a Jew were walking together when they found a gold coin. Since it was difficult to divide one coin among them, they decided to buy with it a cake made of honey, sugar and dates, and to eat the cake together. They bought the cake, but before cutting it up and eating it, the Jew said to his two companions:

'I have a proposal to make. Let us all go to sleep and in the morning each of us will tell what he dreamt. Whoever of us has had the most beautiful dream will have the whole cake all to himself.'

They accepted the idea, placed the cake in a cupboard and went to bed.

As soon as the Jew had made sure that his two companions had fallen into a deep slumber, he got up, went to the cupboard, ate the cake and returned to bed.

When they awoke in the morning, the Jew asked his two companions to relate their dreams. The Muslim said, 'I dreamt that I saw our Prophet Muhammad; he came to me, took me by the hand and led me to paradise, where I saw many beautiful things;' he then went on to describe the beautiful things he saw.

'This is a beautiful dream,' said his two companions.

The Christian was then asked to relate his dream.

He said: 'I dreamt that I saw Jesus come to me; he took me by the hand and led me to hell where he showed me the sinners in torment;' and he proceeded to describe the horrors that he saw.

When the finished, the Jew was asked to describe his dream, and he said, 'As I was asleep, I saw Moses; he awakened me and said, "Your companion the Moslem has gone to heaven; your other companion the Christian has gone to hell; you will not see them again; go and eat the cake." This is what I did.'[44]

AN EXCUSE CAN BE MORE HEINOUS THAN THE CRIME

Abu Nouwas,[45] renowned for his light-hearted verse and sense of humour, was a favourite companion of Caliph Haroun al-Rashid. One day the caliph asked Abu Nouwas to give him a concrete illustration of the proverb 'An excuse can be more heinous than the crime'. Abu Nouwas promised to do so on an early occasion.

In the evening, while walking after dinner through the gardens of the royal palace with the caliph and Queen Zoubeidah, Abu Nouwas pinched the caliph's arm. The caliph was startled and shouted at Abu Nouwas, 'What's this! Are you mad?'

Abu Nouwas excused himself profusely, 'I crave the forgiveness of Your Majesty,' he said. 'I committed a mistake. In the darkness, I mistook your arm for that of the queen!'

'You miserable wretch!' shouted the caliph. 'You will be beheaded for this because your excuse is more heinous than your crime!'

'Sire, I am quite innocent!' cried Abu Nouwas. 'Didn't you this morning ask me to furnish you with a concrete illustration of that proverb?'

The caliph laughed, and accepted the explanation given by Abu Nouwas as an illustration of the proverb.[46]

THE MICE, THE CAT AND THE BELL

Once there was a wicked cat that spread death and terror among the mice. The surviving mice met to discuss the situation and to find some means to escape from the cat's claws. After long deliberation, they adopted what they thought to be an excellent plan: they would hang a small bell in a collar around the cat's neck so that, when the cat moved, the jingle of the bell would give them the alarm, and enable them to run out of reach. The mice acquired a bell and a collar, and asked for a volunteer to hang the bell around the cat's neck. No one came forward. One of them observed, 'The most difficult part still remains to be done,' and this became a popular saying.[47]

THE GOAT WHO ABUSED THE WOLF

A goat was standing on a roof and abusing a wolf who was standing down below. The wolf replied, 'It is not thou who art abusing me, but it is the place whereon thou standest.'[48]

THE WEAKNESS OF THE TESTIMONY

A Christian and a narrator of Islamic tradition[49] happened to be travelling together in the same boat. During the voyage, the Christian

poured himself a cup of wine from a goatskin and drank it. He then refilled the cup, and offered it to the narrator who took it, apparently without thinking and without concern. The Christian said to him, 'This is wine!' The narrator asked him how he knew it was.

The Christian said, 'My servant bought it from a Jew who swore that it was old wine.'

The narrator quickly emptied the cup and told the Christian, 'We, who narrate the tradition of the Prophet, have doubted the testimony of such narrators as Sifian Ibn Ayniyah and Yazeed Ibn Haroun. Do you think for a moment that we would accept as authentic the word of a Christian, on the basis of what is reported to him by his servant, as to what was said to him by a Jew? By God, I drank this cup only because of the weakness in the chain of authorities.'[50]

A LOADED QUESTION

A man relates the following story:

'I was sitting at the table of a certain miser when he took a bread-cake in his hand and said, "People complain that my bread-cakes are small; now what son of a whore is able to eat the whole of one of these bread-cakes?"'[51]

THE TOOTH-EXTRACTOR

A man went to a tooth-extractor and asked him to extract a tooth that was diseased, and the tooth-extractor asked him for a *zuza*[52] in payment. The man said, 'I will not give a whole *zuza*, but only a half.'

Then the tooth-extractor said to him, 'Less than a *zuza* I will not take, but if thou wishest it, and on account of thine honourable position, I will pull out another tooth as well, and I will not charge thee any more than the *zuza*.'[53]

THE VIRTUES OF A MUSLIM

A man once asked Ash'ab, a *raconteur* who lived in Arabia during the eighth century, 'Wouldn't it be more fitting for you to abandon story-telling and instead narrate the *hadith*?[54] Ash'ab replied that he had heard a *hadith* and narrated it. The man asked him what was that *hadith*. Ash'ab replied, 'I haved heard a *hadith* from Nafe' who heard it from the son of Omar who had heard the Prophet say, "Two virtues, if found in a Muslim, make him pure to God."' The man asked what were those two virtues. Ash'ab replied, 'Nafe' forgot one, and I forgot the other.'[55]

THE MAGIC ROPE

Five hundred dinars were stolen from the house of a merchant in Baghdad. Three suspects were arrested and brought to the chief of police, who told the suspects, 'I will not beat you nor subject you to torture in order to discover which of you is the guilty one. I have a magic rope that does the detection work for me. This rope is stretched from one end of a darkened room to the other, and each one of you will enter this room, seize the rope, and pass his hand along its whole length. The rope will wind itself on to the hand of the thief.' Unknown to the suspects, the rope was smeared with black paint.

The suspects were introduced into the darkened room, one after the other. Two of them seized the rope, ran their hands along it, and came out with their hands smeared with the paint. But the third one, fearing the magic rope would detect him as the thief, did not touch it, and came out with his hands unspoiled. This established his guilt and the stolen dinars were found concealed in an old jar in his house.[56]

A DEGRADING RANSOM

In the days when the tribes of Arabia frequently fought against each other, a respectable figure of this time, Abu Hassan al-Ansari, was captured in a raid and taken away prisoner by an enemy tribe. It was a usual practice then, if a prisoner were not killed, to liberate him upon payment of a valuable ransom, the amount of which depended upon his rank and personality. In the case of al-Ansari, however, his captors were more interested in humiliating him and his tribe than in securing financial reward. Accordingly, they did not ask for any sum of money, but declared they would release him for a donkey as ransom.

The members of al-Ansari's tribe were offended, and refused to offer such a degrading ransom. The prisoner, however, sent word to his tribe insisting that they should bring to his captors a donkey as they had asked. When the men of his tribe arrived with the donkey, he told them, 'Give my captors their brother, and take your own,' thus avenging the insult made to him and to his tribe.[57]

THE CAT WHO SAT AS JUDGE AMONG THE MICE

Two mice stole a piece of cheese and, being unable to agree over its division between them, decided to put the case before an old cat, who had long since repented of her ways and given up chasing mice.

'Certainly,' agreed the cat, 'I will divide it fairly for you.'

She took a knife and cut the cheese into two unequal parts. She then placed them in the scales and, finding that they did not balance, cut a piece off the larger part and swallowed it. It was now the other part that was too heavy, so she cut a slice from it and ate it. And so she repeated the process until finally there was only a tiny piece left in one of the scales.

'And this,' she said, gobbling it up, 'is for my fee.'[58]

THE SECRET OF THE CHEST

A locked chest was in the booty brought by an armed expedition returning from a campaign in Persia to al-Hajjaj, the governor of Iraq. The chest had been found among the treasures of the Persian kings. Al-Hajjaj ordered that the lock be broken. When the chest was opened, it was found to contain a small chest which was also locked.

Al-Hajjaj then decided to put the small chest in auction, to be sold to the highest bidder, but on condition that the purchaser would agree to have it opened before taking it away, so that al-Hajjaj would know what was hidden in it. Several people participated in the auction, and the chest was adjudged to the highest bidder, who paid five thousand dinars for it. In accordance with the conditions of the auction, the small chest was then opened. It was found to contain a small piece of

paper on which was written, 'Whoever wants to have a long beard should brush it upwards.'[59]

A MODEL FOR ENGRAVING

Al-Jahez, the most eminent satirical writer in Arabic literature, was very ugly and had protruding eyes. His sense of humour and his love of satire spared no one, even himself. Among his many anecdotes, al-Jahez tells the following story:

A woman once came to me and said, 'I would like you to accompany me to the souq for I have a favour to ask from you.' I accompanied her and she took me to a Jewish goldsmith. Pointing at me, she told the goldsmith, 'Like him!' and went away.

Amazed at the woman's conduct, and much more at her remark, I asked the goldsmith what she meant by saying, 'Like him!'

The goldsmith replied, 'This woman brought to me a stone to set on a ring and asked me to engrave on it the image of a devil, I told her, "My lady, I have never seen the devil." She said, "That is no problem." So she went off and brought you!'[60]

THE MAN WAS NOT SO MAD AFTER ALL!

A madman went up to a polished pillar and said, 'Who will give me a *zuza* for going up to the top?' And when several folk had given him a coin, he said, 'Now bring me a ladder.'

The people said, 'Did we agree with thee to climb the pillar using a ladder?'

The madman said, 'Ye certainly did not agree with me to do it without one: ye only stipulated that I should go up!'[61]

THE BLIND MAN'S LANTERN

A story told by Djamy, a Persian mystic writer:

It so happened that one night a blind man, who carried a clay jar on his shoulder and a lantern in his hand, met an interfering man in the common thoroughfare. This meddlesome character stopped the blind man and jeered at him, saying, 'Thou ignorant blind man! Nights and days are the same to thee, and light and darkness equal to thee: of what use is this lantern to thee?'

The blind man laughed and said, 'This lamp is not for me. It is for such people as thou – thoughtless, blind-hearted idiots – so that they should not bump into me and break my jar!'[62]

SOLVING A KNOTTY PROBLEM

Under Islamic law a wife is divorced by her husband's repudiation with the words: 'I divorce you' or 'you are divorced'.

The story is told of a woman who was able to resolve a difficult situation on the spot and to thwart her husband's intended repudiation by her quick and ingenious mind. This occurred when her husband, seeing his wife one day climbing on a ladder told her, 'You are divorced if you climb up the ladder, you are divorced if you come down the steps of the ladder, you are divorced if you remain where you are.' In this fashion the husband thought that he had put his wife in a fix from which she should not be able to escape.

But the wife easily solved the knotty problem: she neither ascended nor descended the steps of the ladder. Neither did she remain motionless. She simply jumped all the way down.[63]

THE SOURCE OF AN OBLIGATION

An Arab from the desert entered upon Emir Khaled Ben Abdallah at a time when his door was not attended by an usher, nor were any of his retinue about. Khaled asked the man where he came from, and the man replied that he came from the Tamin Arabs. The emir then observed, 'No kinship exists between us that warrants the liberty you have taken to enter without permission, and no bond ties us that imposes on us any obligation towards you.'

The bedouin said, 'But yes, you do owe me an obligation!'

'And what is this obligation?' inquired the emir.

'The obligation arises from my seeking you for help and assistance, from my treading on your carpet, and from the trust and high hopes I have founded on you!'

'By God,' replied the Emir, 'this is an obligation that falls upon free men. Sit down and do not be alarmed.'

The emir then ordered his servant to pay to the bedouin 'one thousand', without specifying whether he meant a thousand dinars[64] or a thousand dirhems.[65] The servant brought one thousand *dirhems* and handed them to the bedouin. However, the latter refused to take them, and told the servant that the Emir was too generous to order the payment to him of fewer than one thousand dinars, and he would not leave without taking the full amount. The emir, who witnessed the incident, laughed and said to his servant, 'Give the man a thousand dinars: he deserves this sum for his having thought so well of us!'[66]

PUNISHMENT FOR DRINKING WINE

The drinking of wine is forbidden by the Islamic religion, and the punishment ordained for a breach of such prohibition is the administration of eighty lashes. This punishment was administered on several occasions by the governor of Medina to Ibn Harmeh, a poet who was addicted to drinking, and was often found drunk in the streets of the city. Infuriated by the governor's severity towards him, Ibn Harmeh decided to appeal to Caliph Abu Ja'far al-Mansour.[67]

When he appeared before the caliph he recited a poem in his praise, and the caliph was greatly pleased. The caliph asked him what he desired for a reward. Ibn Harmeh replied that he did not want a monetary reward, but simply a letter from the caliph to the governor of Medina ordering that he, Ibn Harmeh, should not be lashed for his drinking. The caliph said that this was something he could not do. He could not exempt him from a punishment ordained by the law. However, he would do something else: he would order the governor of Medina to administer one hundred lashes to anyone who brought to him Ibn Harmeh in a drunken condition, and to administer eighty lashes to Ibn Harmeh himself in accordance with the law.

And so it happened that when Ibn Harmeh, drunken and happy, met the police in the streets of Medina, he would ask defiantly and loudly, 'Who will buy one hundred lashes for eighty?'[68]

THE PRICE OF HOSPITALITY

Bedouin hospitality is proverbial. But it is a hospitality mixed with great pride, as is shown by the following story.

Two travellers crossing a desert were caught in a violent sand-storm, and they sought refuge in the encampment of a bedouin. The bedouin welcomed his guests and slaughtered a camel for them to eat.[69]

On the following day he slaughtered for them another camel. The guests gently remonstrated with him for doing this and reminded him that they had eaten very little of the animal he had killed for them on the preceding day. The bedouin dismissed their protest. 'I don't feed my guests on what is left over from the day before,' he told them proudly.

And so while the two travellers stayed as his guests, the bedouin killed for them one camel each day. When the storm abated, they decided to depart but found that their host was absent. They asked the bedouin's wife to thank her husband for his hospitality to them and to present their excuses to him for leaving before his return. They then gave her a bag that contained one hundred dinars as an expression of their gratitude and left on their journey.

A few hours later the two travellers heard the shouts of a man running behind them with a spear in his hand and calling upon them to stop. When he reached them, they recognized their host. Shaking with anger, he threw to them the bag of money and said menacingly, 'You vile people, you have dared to give us the price of our hospitality! Take your money back or I'll transpierce you with this spear!' The two travellers took back their one hundred dinars and went away regret-ting their *faux pas*.[70]

THE BEGGAR'S ADVICE

A beggar knocked on the door of a house and asked for charity. The people of the house gave him nothing and said to him, 'May God help you.'[71] The beggar then asked for a piece of bread, and received the same reply. He asked for a little flour, or some corn, or some barley. The reply was that these people had none. He then begged for a drink of water, but was told that the household had not one drop of it. Greatly angered, the beggar said to the people of the house, 'What are you sitting here for? Get up and go around begging, for you are in greater need of charity than I am!'[72]

A WHOLE LOAF

A blind beggar of Isfahan was given once a loaf of bread by a passer-by. The beggar invoked God's blessings upon his benefactor in these words: 'May God Almighty be benevolent to you, may He bless you, may He reward you, and may He return you to your country, safe and sound.'

The man who had given the loaf was intrigued by the beggar's invocations, and he asked him, 'How did you guess I was a stranger away from his home?'

The beggar replied, 'I have now been begging in this city for the last twenty years, and no one has ever given me a whole loaf.'[73]

RENT INCREASE

Al-Jahez in *al-Bukhala'* tells many humorous tales about the misers of his time. Each one of his anecdotes is a character study; the work is one of the masterpieces of Arabic literature. One of his anecdotes is about a man called al-Kindi, and his exactions as a landlord. The story is told by a tenant of al-Kindi in these words:

While I was living in al-Kindi's house, a cousin of mine and his son came to stay with me. No sooner had they arrived, than I received a note from my landlord which stated, 'If the period during which your two visitors intend to stay does not exceed one or two days, I shall endure this; nevertheless, if tenants are going to take the liberty of inviting guests to stay overnight, it will not be long before they inflict them on us for long periods.'

'They are only staying about a month,' I hastened to reply.

He wrote back, 'The rent of your house is thirty dirhems; and since there are six of you, that comes to five dirhems a head. Now that there are two more of you, that will be another ten dirhems; so from today your rent will be forty dirhems.'

'What harm does their being here do you?' I asked him in reply. 'Their weight presses only on the earth, which supports mountains, and their board is entirely my responsibility. Write and let me know your reasons.'

Little did I know the storm I was raising, or the road I was setting out on! He sent me a letter as follows:

'There are several reasons that prompt me to adopt this attitude: they are well known, and do not alter. The first is that the cesspit fills up more quickly, and it costs a lot to have it emptied. Then, as the number of feet increases, there is more trading on the clay-surfaced flat roofs and the plastered floors of the bedrooms, and more wear and tear on the staircase: the clay flakes off, the plaster crumbles, and the steps get worn down: to say nothing of the fact that the ceiling joists bend and break under all this trampling on them and the extra weight they have to bear. When people are continually going in and out, opening and closing doors and drawing and shooting the bolt, the doors split and their fastenings get broken off. When there are more children, and twice as big a swarm of brats, the nails and hinges of the doors get torn off, and all the courtyards suffer; the children dig holes in them for their nutshell games, and crack the flagstones with their go-carts. Moreover the walls get ruined through people hammering in pegs and shelf-brackets . . . (The indictment goes on and on and then concludes):

'Now we have made it clear to you that visitors must be regarded as permanent residents, and that each additional guest warrants an increase in rent. If, my dear fellow, I closed my eyes to two extra people, I wager you would soon impose on me the continual presence of outsiders in your house; the rent would be the same for a thousand people as for one, and visitors would come and go, and occupy and vacate the house, without me being a penny the richer.

'Moreover if I had not asked you for the extra rent, and had not acquainted you with the obligation, my indulgence would not have been appreciated: for you do not understand the importance that attaches to an increase in the number of tenants. A poet of bygone days said on this subject,

Ingratitude makes one weary of being charitable;

and another said:

I received ingratitude in exchange for my charity: sometimes the ungrateful are those whose charity has not been appreciated.'[74]

THE POET'S REWARD

The Arabs have always been admirers of poetry and many tales are told of poems composed in praise of kings, ministers and governors, and of the huge rewards given to their authors.

The story is told of a king who combined shrewdness with an extraordinary memory to the extent that he was capable, after hearing a poem only once, of repeating it word for word as if he had known it before. His usher could also repeat the poem after having heard it recited twice, that is, by the poet and by his master. The king had also a slave girl who was trained to repeat any poem after hearing it recited by the poet, the king and the usher.

The king was extremely avaricious. Whenever a poet came to him to recite a poem composed in his praise, he would tell him, 'If your poem is a piece of trite and hackneyed verse, you will receive no reward; but if it is an original poem which we have not heard before, we shall give you its weight in gold.'

And so when the poet recited his poem, the king, hearing it once, would memorize it, regardless of the number of its verses, and would tell its author, 'This is not an original poem. We have heard it before', and he would then recite it to the dumbfounded author without fault or hesitation.

If the poet protested that the poem was his original composition, the king would tell him, 'Our usher also knows this poem,' and he would ask the usher to recite it. The usher, having heard it twice, would repeat it word for word. If the poet still entertained any doubt and showed any sign of disbelief, the king would say to him, 'Even our slave girl who is behind this screen knows it,' and he would ask his slave girl to recite the poem from behind the screen. Having heard it three times, the slave girl would also recite the poem. Seeing this, the poet would go away muddle-headed, completely baffled, and almost doubting his sanity.

Al-Asma'i[75] knew the king's rare capacity to repeat a poem after hearing it once, but he decided to overcome this difficulty and to make a bid for the king's reward. He composed a poem full of unused and unusual words, so that neither the king, nor his usher, nor his slave girl, would be able to memorize and repeat it. He then went to the king's palace disguised as a bedouin, and asked to be introduced into the king's presence. When he was brought before the king, he said, 'Sire, I have composed a poem in your praise and I crave leave to recite it to you.'

The king told him, 'We shall listen to it, but you know the condition: if we have heard it before, you will receive no reward, but if we have not heard it before, you will receive its weight in gold.' The poet said, 'I accept the conditions,' and he recited his poem. When he finished, the king was unable to repeat it because of its complexity. He looked at his usher, but from the vacant expression on his face he could judge his inability also to repeat it. He shouted at his slave girl behind the screen to repeat the poem, but there was a complete and significant silence.

The king then said to the poet, 'You have spoken the truth. This is an original poem which we have not heard before. You shall have your reward. Give to our treasurer the piece of paper on which it is written and he will give you its weight in gold.'

The poet replied: 'Sire, the poem is not written on paper as I could not find any paper to write it upon. But I had a piece of a marble column that had been lying in my house since my father died, and I carved the poem upon it.' He then went and unloaded from the saddle bag on his mount a chunk of marble of sizeable dimensions, and presented it to the king. The marble was weighed, and it was found that all the gold in the king's treasury was insufficient to pay the poet's reward. The poet, however, accepted a generous gift by way of compromise.[76]

A ZEALOUS SERVANT

A man had a servant who was lazy, both physically and mentally. He sent him one day to the souq to buy some figs and grapes. The servant spent a long time on the errand and when he eventually returned he brought the grapes but not the figs. His master scolded and beat him and said, 'From now on, if I send you on one errand you should do two errands at the same time, not as you have done today.'

On the following day the master fell ill, and he ordered his servant to hurry and call a doctor for him. The servant rushed out, and returned with the doctor and another man. The master looked at the two men and asked his servant, 'This doctor, I understand, but who is the other man you brought with him?'

The servant replied, 'May God Almighty help me. Didn't you beat me yesterday and tell me that when you send me on one errand I should perform two errands? Well, this is exactly what I have done.

You sent me to fetch a doctor, and I brought you a doctor. At the same time, I brought the other man, who is a gravedigger, so that if the doctor does not cure you, the other man will dig your grave. What are you now complaining about?'[77]

THE THIEF'S PROFIT

Two thieves stole a donkey, and one of them drove it to the souq to sell it. On the way he met a man, who carried a tray containing some fish. The man with the tray asked the thief if his donkey were for sale. As he replied in the affirmative, the man with the tray said to him, 'Will you hold this tray for me while I try the animal?'

The thief took the tray and held it, while the would-be buyer rode the donkey to and fro, sometimes at speed, and sometimes slowing down, but always riding farther and farther away. Then finally, he turned into a side street and disappeared from the thief's view. The thief awaited the man's return with rising anxiety. Then, as he did not return, he searched for him everywhere but could find no trace of him or the donkey. When the thief realized that the other man had deceived him and stolen the donkey, he returned, discomfited, to his companion with the tray and the fish. His companion asked him, 'What have you done with the donkey? Have you sold it?' 'Yes,' replied the thief. 'For how much?' asked his companion. 'I sold it at cost, and this tray with the fish is the profit,' was the reply.[78]

THE JUDGE WAS ANGERED BY THE SETTLEMENT

A young fox met an old fox and said to him, 'Teach me some of the tricks of our brotherhood.' The older fox said, 'I know a hundred tricks. Follow me and you will learn some of them.' So the young fox decided to keep his elder company, in the hope of learning some of his stratagems.

The two foxes then set out together on a prowling expedition, and in the course of their journey the young fox asked his companion, 'What do we do if we meet a lion?'

The other replied, 'Don't you worry. If we meet one, I shall show you how to deal with him.'

The old fox had hardly finished speaking those words when a lion suddenly sprang up before them. The lion asked them, 'Where are you heading for?'

The old fox replied, 'We were, in fact, looking for Your Majesty.'

The lion asked, 'What for?'

The fox replied, 'Our father died, and left us some young sheep. We quarrelled over their division between us because my brother here wanted more than his share. So I said to him, "Let us go to our venerable lord and master, the king of animals, and ask him to divide the inheritance equitably between us."' The lion decided that he would not kill and eat the two foxes as he thought that the sheep might be more appetizing than the two emaciated foxes.

'Where are the sheep?' he asked hungrily.

'They are in this garden,' replied the fox, pointing to a garden with high walls nearby.

'If it pleases Your Majesty,' said the fox, 'my brother will go and bring the sheep over to you.'

The lion accepted the suggestion, and the young fox was asked to hurry and fetch the sheep out from the garden. The young fox ran and entered the garden through a narrow water channel in the wall, and disappeared from view.

Time passed, and the young fox did not return. Noticing the lion's impatience, the old fox said to him, 'I told Your Majesty that my brother was wicked and does not want a fair and equitable division of our inheritance. With your permission, I shall go and bring him back along with the sheep.' The lion agreed, but as he was getting more hungry every minute he told the fox to hurry.

The fox did not need to be told to hurry. He rushed to the garden which he entered through the narrow water channel, climbed on the wall and shouted to the lion, 'Your Majesty can now go away in peace as my brother and I have settled the dispute between us.'

Hearing these words, the lion roared with anger, and struck his tail violently against the ground. The fox feigned surprise, and said to the lion, 'My brother and I set you up as a judge between us, and I have never known a judge to be angered as you are by a settlement between the parties.'

Thereupon, he jumped back into the safety of the garden under the admiring eyes of his brother fox, who had never seen such a clever trick before.[79]

A RESEMBLANCE IS EXPLAINED

A story told by Obeid Zakani, the Persian writer:

A man by the name of Khalaf was the governor of Khurasan. He was told that there lived in his domain a man who was his exact replica in both features and manners. He ordered this man to be brought before him, and asked him, 'Was your mother in the habit of going to the houses of the great for service or as a go-between?'

The man answered, 'My mother, may Allah rest her soul in peace, was a poor and unpretentious woman who never left her home, but my father served in the houses of the great as a water carrier.'[80]

RECOMPENSE AND PUNISHMENT

Muhammad Ibrahim Mawsulli recounted that he and his companion came upon a bedouin encampment during their travels. There they found an exceedingly ugly man, with squinting eyes and a long white beard, beating his wife, who was as beautiful as a dream. As Muhammad and his companions rushed to stop the man from beating his wife, she said to them 'Leave him alone, he has done a good deed in the eyes of God, and I have committed a sin, and God made of me his recompense, and made of him my punishment.'[81]

A THOUGHTFUL THIEF

I have never seen a more thoughtful person, said Imam Shafe'i,[82] than a thief who stole my shoes while I was praying at the mosque.[83] He took them away from my side while I was looking at him, and I said nothing as I did not wish to interrupt my prayers. He then went to my home and told my family, 'The imam addresses to you his greetings and would like you to send him a pair of shoes, as his own were stolen at the mosque.' Then, as I was still at the mosque, barefooted,

wondering how to return home, my servant arrived with a pair of shoes and informed me of what had happened.[84]

CONTAINED BY WORDS

A man bought a new house and he and his family had hardly moved into it than a beggar stopped at the door, and asked for charity. The owner said to him: 'May God help you!' The beggar went away.

Soon afterwards, a second beggar stopped at the door and asked for alms. He was dismissed in the same fashion. Then a third beggar came along, and was turned away with the same phrase. Thereupon, the owner of the house remarked to his daughter, 'How numerous are the beggars in this neighbourhood?'

'Father,' replied the daughter, 'so long as you are able to contain them with words, why worry about their number?'[85]

WHAT SHOULD ONE BELIEVE?

A man stole a cockerel and hid it under his coat. The owner caught up with him and asked, 'What are you doing with my cockerel?'

The thief began to swear that he had never touched the bird, but the owner, looking at its tail protruding from the man's coat, said, 'Shall I believe your oath or the tail of the cock?'[86]

THE EMIR'S GIFT

The story is told of a poet who composed a poem in praise of a certain

emir. The poem was more remarkable for its humour than for its literary quality. After the author had recited his poem, the emir, wanting to be facetious, ordered an unusual reward to be given to the poet: a donkey's saddle. The poet showed no reaction: he merely put the saddle across his shoulders, thanked the emir, and went away.

In the street, he met one of his friends, who was intrigued by the strange sight of him carrying a donkey's saddle across his shoulders. The friend asked him, 'What is happening here?' The poet explained, 'I praised our lord the emir with my best verse, and he made me a gift of his choicest garment!'[87]

THE TESTIMONY OF DONKEYS

There was in Mecca a man who unlawfully kept a wineshop. Complaints were made to the governor who had him exiled to a place outside the city. The wine merchant moved his business to his new abode, and informed his clients that they could reach him easily and cheaply by riding a donkey to his new establishment. His business flourished, and donkeys for hire were in great demand by customers of the wineshop.

Complaints were again made to the governor about the wine-drinking that was going on outside the city. The governor asked for proof. Those who complained said that they could not produce eye-witnesses, but suggested to the governor that he order the donkeys available for hire in the city to be gathered in one place and then released; by force of habit the donkeys were sure to head directly for the wineshop.

The governor accepted the suggestion and ordered that all the donkeys available for hire should be gathered in one spot and then

turned loose. Sure enough, the donkeys unerringly went to the wineshop as if they had been led there by hand. On the strength of this evidence, the wine merchant was arrested and brought before the governor who sentenced him to receive eighty lashes as punishment for his offence. As the guards seized the wine merchant to take him away and administer the punishment, he shouted that he wished to say something. Addressing the governor, he said, 'May God protect you. I think your decision is a big mistake which you may regret in the future. I do not fear the punishment you have ordered as much as I fear that people will make a laughing-stock of you for having based your sentence on the testimony of donkeys!' The governor laughed and ordered the release of this witty offender.[88]

WHO DESERVED INTERDICTION?

A rich and influential man in Basra built a palace, which stood near a ruined house that was owned by an old woman. The rich man wanted to remove from his neighbourhood the displeasing sight of the old woman's house.

The house was not worth more than twenty dinars, but, to tempt the woman to sell, the rich man offered her two hundred dinars for it. The old woman refused the offer because she did not want to sell her home.

People said to her, 'You refuse two hundred dinars for what is worth only twenty? The qadi will interdict[89] you for your foolishness!'

But the old woman replied, 'Why would the qadi interdict not one who offers two hundred dinars for what is worth only twenty?'[90]

THE SLAVE GIRL'S REVENGE

It is said that a certain king was inflamed with the love of women and neglected the affairs of his kingdom. His vizier counselled him ceaselessly to change his mode of life, and to abandon his passion for the other sex. When the vizier's counsels bore fruit, the king's favourite slave girl observed a great change in her master's attitude towards her. He began to show little interest in her dancing or singing, or even in her favours. So she asked what had come over him. The king admitted to her that his vizier had prevailed upon him to give up his imprudent passion for women. Greatly angered to learn that the vizier was the cause of her misfortune, the slave girl said to the king, 'My Lord, give me away as a present to your vizier, and I shall show you what I shall do to him.' Having lost interest in her himself and being curious to know what would happen, the king donated his slave girl to his vizier. The vizier took her to his house, and was soon captivated by her charm and beauty. But the young woman did not encourage his philandering, and insisted on one condition: she would not grant him her favours unless he let her ride on his back, and promenade her around the courtyard of his house.

At first, the vizier resisted this strange and outlandish request, but his infatuation for the young woman soon overcame his opposition and, eventually, he consented to do what she asked. So at an appointed time, the vizier went down on all fours, and the young woman placed a saddle over his back, and a bridle around his neck, and then rode him around the courtyard of the house, emitting shrill cries of joy. At that very moment, the king, who had secretly been warned in advance by his slave girl of what was to happen, appeared on the scene, and was flabbergasted by the extraordinary sight of his vizier serving as a

docile mount for his slave girl. The king severely rebuked the vizier for his undignified behaviour, and said to him, 'For years you have remonstrated with me about my love for women, and here you have allowed yourself to be ridden like a donkey by one of them!'

'Sire,' replied the vizier, who had quickly recovered his wits, 'this is precisely what I feared would befall you!'[91]

IT IS QUALITY RATHER THAN QUANTITY WHICH COUNTS

A fox taunted a lioness, and mocked her because she only gave birth to one cub a year.

'Very true,' observed the lioness, 'but he is a lion.'[92]

WHY THE MAN APPEARED GREAT IN THE KING'S EYES

Al-Sha'bi[93] said:

Abdul Malek[94] sent me on a mission to the king of the Greeks. When I met the king, and he noticed, during our discussion, the strength and cogency of my arguments, he asked me whether I belonged to the ruling family of the caliphs. I replied, 'No, I am just one of the people.' He then wrote a note, sealed it and gave it to me to deliver to Abdul Malek.

When I returned, I gave the note to Abdul Malek. He read it, and then asked me, 'Do you know its contents?' I replied that I did not.

Abdul Malek said, 'The note expresses astonishment that a people who have among them a man like you should have chosen someone else to rule over them. Do you know what was his intention in writing this note to me?'

I replied that I did not.

Abdul Malek said, 'He envied me for having you in my service, and he wanted me to kill you.'

I said, 'O Commander of the Faithful, the only reason that I appeared great in his eyes was that he had not seen you!'[95]

CHOSROËS AND SHIREEN

A wise man said, 'The counsel of women can be costly.' This was proved by the story of a king of Persia named Chosroës, who followed the advice of his wife, queen Shireen.

The king loved fish, and one day a fisherman caught an enormous fish which he offered to the king. The king was so pleased with the present that he ordered a reward of four thousand dirhems to be given to the fisherman. The queen witnessed this liberality with surprise, and when the fisherman had gone, she reproached the king for what she described to be unwise squandering of a large sum of money.

'If tomorrow,' she said to him, 'you were to reward an important member of your court with a similar sum, he would scorn the gift, and say that his standing in your eyes was no higher than that of a fisherman!'

The king replied, 'You are right. But it would be shameful for the king to go back on his reward, and the thing is done now.'

The queen said to him, 'What you have done can be undone and I shall show you a way.'

The king inquired, 'How?'

The queen said, 'All you have to do is to order the fisherman to be brought back, and then you should ask him, "Is this fish male or female?" If he says it is male, then you will tell him that you wanted a

female. And if he tells you it is female, then you will tell him that you wanted a male. In this way you will recover the money back from him.'

The king followed the queen's advice, and ordered that the fisherman be brought before him. When the fisherman came, the king asked him, 'Is this fish male or female?' The fisherman, who had a quick mind, kissed the ground before the king, and said, 'May God preserve the king. This fish is neither male nor female. It is hermaphrodite!'

On hearing the fisherman's answer, the king burst into laughter, and, being delighted with the fisherman's sense of humour, ordered that another sum of four thousand dirhems be given to him as a reward. The fisherman took the money, put it in a bag and carried it away on his shoulder.

As he was leaving, a coin fell from the bag. The fisherman put down the bag, picked up the coin and placed it back in the bag. All this time the king and queen were observing what he was doing. The queen then said to the king, 'Have you seen the meanness of this man? He drops a dirhem and he puts down his bag to pick it up, instead of leaving it for one of your servants, or for a poor man who will invoke God's blessings on your head!'

The king said, 'You are right,' and he ordered that the fisherman be brought back.

When the fisherman appeared before him the king said to him, 'You are no man! You are mean and contemptible! You have put down this bag full of money and stooped down to pick up a paltry dirhem, instead of leaving it to one of the servants! You should be ashamed of yourself!' The fisherman kissed the ground in front of the king and said to him, 'I did not pick up the dirhem out of meanness, I picked it up because the king's effigy is engraved on it, and I feared that someone, without seeing it, would tread on it with his shoe. This would have been an affront to the king, and an outrage to his name and image of which I would have been the cause!' The king was seized with admiration for this remarkable explanation and, in appreciation, ordered that the fisherman be rewarded with another four thousand dirhems.

But at the same time the king ordered that the town-crier proclaim publicly all around the city, 'Whoever listens to the counsel of women will be the loser.'[96]

SURPASSED IN GENEROSITY

Generosity is a virtue highly esteemed among the Arabs. Mi'an Ibn Zayideh, a famous Arab emir who lived during the eighth century, and died in AD 768, was famed for his generosity and eulogized for this virtue by the poets of his time. However, he was outdone in this regard by a man of humble means, and he tells the following story:

When Caliph al-Mansour ordered my arrest and set a reward for my capture, I decided to escape to the desert. As I, in disguise on my camel, left one of the gates of Baghdad, a black man carrying a sword followed me. When we were out of the view of the city guards, he grabbed the camel's bridle, forced the animal down to its knees, and seized me by the arm.

'What do you want?' I asked him.

'You are Mi'an Ibn Zayideh, the man wanted by the Commander of the Faithful,' he replied.

I protested and said, 'Fear God, I am a stranger here.'

But he dismissed my protest, clung to me and would not let me go. When I saw that he was quite serious, and he was not going to release me, I said to him, 'You will not derive any great benefit by delivering me to the caliph. I shall give you a much greater reward. Here, take the necklace, which is worth several times the amount of the caliph's reward, and do not be the cause of the shedding of my blood.'

As I spoke these words, I produced a beautiful necklace made of precious stones and offered it to him. He looked at the jewel for a moment and then said, 'You have not lied about its value, but I shall not let you go until you answer a question I wish to put to you. If you answer it truthfully, I shall set you free.'

'What is your question?' I asked.

He said: 'You are famed for your generosity, but tell me: have you ever given away the whole of your fortune?'

I said, 'No.'

He then asked whether I had given away one-tenth of my fortune. I felt ashamed and said, 'Yes.' He then said, 'This is not much. My monthly pay from the caliph is twenty dirhems, and I do not own on the face of this earth possessions worth one hundred dirhems. And here I am donating to you this necklace which is worth several thousand dirhems, and I am sparing your life despite the caliph's reward. I am doing so because I want you to know that God has created men who are more generous than you! I also want you to feel less proud of yourself and to look down after today with contempt upon every charitable deed you have done.'

I said, 'Man, you cover me with shame. The shedding of my blood is easier to me than what you have done. I beseech you, take this necklace.' He laughed and said, 'You want to belie and disprove my words. By God, I shall not take the necklace nor accept a price for a good deed,' and he disappeared.

Ever since, I have been searching for him, and I am offering a reward to whomsoever should find him, but without avail.[97]

THE THIEF'S HONOUR

Osman Khayat was a thief with a code of honour. He would teach the members of his gang to observe three rules: never to steal from a neighbour; to respect women; and never to treat the victim otherwise than as an equal partner.

One night, he and his gang were lying in wait on the outskirts of Baghdad, hoping to rob passers-by, when a distinguished-looking young man came by. The young man saluted the thieves: 'Peace be on you,' he said, and some of them replied, 'And peace be on you.'[98]

Then some of the thieves moved forward to seize him and divest him of his money and other belongings, but they were angrily ordered back by their chief who said to them,' This young man saluted you in order to gain his safety, and you have returned his salute. By returning his salute, you have pledged yourselves to assure his peace and safety.'

The members of the gang said, 'Then we shall let him go.'

Their chief said, 'This is not enough. I am afraid that others may harm him. I want three of you to accompany him, and to make sure that he reaches his house in safety.'

Three of the gang accompanied the young man, and on reaching his house, he gave them a sum of money in appreciation of what they had done. When they returned, and their chief learned of what had happened, he flew into a rage at them.

'This is worse than robbing him in the first instance!' he shouted. 'How dare you take money for discharging an obligation and honouring a pledge? Go back straight away and return the money to him.'[99]

HE WAS TAUGHT THREE QUALITIES

A man hired a porter to carry for him a crate full of glass flasks, and by way of remuneration offered to teach him three qualities that would be of benefit to him. The porter accepted the terms. When the porter had covered one-third of the way, he said to the owner of the crate, 'Teach me the first quality.' The man said, 'Here it is. If anyone tells you that hunger is better than eating one's fill, do not believe him.' The porter nodded in agreement.

When they reached two-thirds of the way, the porter said to the owner of the crate, 'Let me now have the second.' The man said, 'Here is the second. If anyone tells you that walking is better than riding, do not believe him.' The porter again nodded.

When they reached the man's house, the porter said, 'Let me have the third.'

The owner of the crate said, 'Here is the third. If anyone tells you that there exists a porter more stupid than you, do not believe him.'

Thereupon the porter threw down the crate on the ground, smashing the flasks to smithereens, and said to the man, 'If anyone tells you that a single flask in this crate has remained unbroken, do not believe him at all!'[100]

IMPRISONMENT OF THE CREDITOR

A man sued his debtor before the qadi. The debtor admitted that he owed the plaintiff twenty-four dirhems. The qadi said to the debtor, 'Why don't you pay back to the plaintiff what you owe him?'

The debtor replied, 'I own a donkey and make my living by

carrying loads on it. I earn four dirhems a day from my work. I spend one dirhem to feed the donkey, and one dirhem on my own food. This leaves me two dirhems each day to pay off my creditor. When at the end of twelve days I have saved enough to settle my debt, I start looking for my creditor to pay him, but I do not find him. The result is that I spend the amount that I have saved on other things.'

'What do you expect me to do?', asked the judge of the debtor.

'Your Honour,' said the debtor, 'as I never have twenty dirhems at one time in my pocket, there is no way for me to pay off my debt, except if you were to order the plaintiff to be imprisoned for a period of twelve days so that I would know where to find him when I have saved the amount needed to pay him off!'[101]

THE NEIGHBOUR'S OATH

A woman sued a man before the judge of Basra to recover an object she had left with him in trust and which the defendant denied having received. The judge had newly been appointed to his office and his knowledge of the law was neither deep nor extensive. As the woman had no evidence to prove her claim, the judge told her she could, if she wished, tender the oath to the defendant.[102] To this the plaintiff objected, and told the judge, 'You cannot possibly ask the defendant to swear the oath regarding my claim. He has no scruples, and he will take the oath without hesitation, and I shall lose my right. Instead ask Ishaq Ben Souweid, who is his neighbour, to take the oath!' The judge accepted the plaintiff's foolish request and sent for the neighbour and administered to him the oath![103]

THE ODOUR OF HOPES

A poor man said to his wife, 'I wish someone would make us a present of a sheep; we would roast it and make a delicious meal of it.'

A woman neighbour overheard the last part of the conversation, and imagined that her neighbours were, in fact, planning to roast a sheep for their evening meal. So, hoping to be invited to partake of the feast she thought to be in preparation, she waited until supper time, and then went and knocked on her neighbours' door. When the door was opened, she said, 'I was drawn here by the odour of your roast sheep.'

On hearing these words, the man said to his wife, 'If our neighbours can smell the odour of our hopes, let us quickly move away from this neighbourhood!'[104]

A VISIT TO A SICK MAN

A man learned that one of his friends had fallen sick. Being an invalid himself and unable to visit him, he felt it his duty to send his son to inquire of his friend's health. As the son was a simpleton, the father took care to instruct him on the proper performance of his mission.

'My son,' said he, 'when you enter the patient's room, go and sit near him and ask him, "How are you feeling today?" If he says, "I am well, or I am better", then you say "God be praised". You should then ask him what medicine he takes, and if he says, "This or that", you reply, "This is good for your health." Finally, you will inquire about the physician who attends him, and if he says, "So and so", your comments should be, "You are in good hands."'

The son went to the patient's home, and as he feared he might on the way forget what his father had told him to say, he kept repeating the remarks he was supposed to make in conversation with the sick man, until he mastered them completely. When he arrived, he was introduced into the patient's room, and moved to sit near him. In doing so, he clumsily upset a table and all the medicine bottles that were on it over the sick man. This was sufficient to irritate the patient and worsen his condition, and so when the visitor asked him, 'How are you feeling today?' he replied, 'I am on the verge of death!' Vividly remembering the first comment that his father had asked him to make, the visitor said, 'God be praised!'

The patient became indignant, but before he could open his mouth in protest, his visitor asked him, 'What medicine do you take for your ailment?'

'The poison of death!' replied the sick man with increasing irritation.

'This is good for your health!' interjected the visitor.

Choked with anger, the patient could not utter a sound. The visitor then asked him, 'Who is your physician?' The patient managed to shriek in reply, 'The Angel of Death!'[105] 'You are in good hands!' the visitor assured him, and thereupon departed with the satisfaction of having duly discharged his mission.[106]

THE BLIND MAN'S LOAF

A man worshipped God for seventy years. One day, however, he was tempted by a beautiful woman, and he lived in sin with her for seven days. He then awoke to the realization that he had wasted seventy years of worship for seven days of sin, and he left the woman and went out into the wilderness to repent.

After roaming for some time, he reached, tired and hungry, an old ruined building in which lived ten blind men. He asked for something to eat. But they had no food for him as their daily sustenance was assured by a hermit, who lived nearby and who sent them every evening ten loaves of bread.

When the loaves of bread were brought that evening, the visitor snatched one of them. But the blind man who was left without his loaf asked, 'Where is my loaf?' and began moaning. The visitor was moved and felt that if one of them should go hungry, it should be himself because he was in sin, and so, despite his great hunger, he gave the loaf to the blind man.

During the night, the visitor was on the point of dying and the Angel of Death came to fetch his soul.

Thereupon the Angels of Torment and the Angels of Mercy disputed possession of his soul, the former claiming that he was in sin while the latter claimed that he had repented. The angels were inspired by God to weigh in the scale of justice the man's worship during seventy years against his living in sin for seven days. This was done and it was found that the man's sin outweighed his worship of seventy years. Then the angels were inspired by God to weigh the sin of the seven days against his giving the loaf of bread to the blind man to save his life, although he risked his own. This was done and it was found that his giving the loaf of bread outweighed the sin. So the Angels of Mercy took his soul and God accepted his repentance.[107]

HIS TRUST IN HIS NEIGHBOUR

As a result of a severe drought that befell Iraq, many people faced destitution and famine, and left the country during the emergency to eke out a livelihood elsewhere. A neighbour of Ibn Obeidillah was one of those who decided to leave, but his wife was unable to accompany him on account of her poor health.

When the husband was about to leave, his wife asked him, 'While you are away, who will provide for us?'

The husband replied, 'Our neighbour, Ibn Obeidillah, owes me a debt and I have here a legal document to prove it. Take it to him, and when he reads it he will provide you with what you need until my return.' The husband gave to his wife a piece of paper on which he had written a few lines of poetry and then left.

Some days later the wife went to Ibn Obeidillah and informed him that her husband had gone away on account of the drought, and would be absent for some time. She then repeated to him what her husband had said to her before he left, and presented to him the piece of paper. Ibn Obeidillah looked at it and found written on it the following lines of poetry:

> *As she saw the camels saddled,*
> *and felt the grief of impending separation,*
> *She asked: whom can I rely upon*
> *in this famine when you are gone?*
> *I replied: You have God and*
> *your protector Ibn Obeidillah.*

Ibn Obeidillah said to the wife, 'What your husband told you is correct,' and he assured her means of livelihood until her husband's return.[108]

TWO EMBARRASSING SITUATIONS

Al-Ma'moun is reported to have confided to one of his friends the following story:

I was never so embarrassed in my life as I was in two situations in which I found myself completely unable to speak or reply.

The first occurred when the people of Kufa submitted a complaint against their governor, and I sat down to hear it. I said to them, 'If you are all going to speak one after the other, it will be tiresome. Choose one of your number to speak for you all, and we shall then discuss the matter together.'

They replied, 'We have already chosen a spokesman, and if the Commander of the Faithful will hear him, he will speak for us all.'

So one of them came forward and spoke in these words, 'O Commander of the Faithful, the man you have appointed to govern us for the last three years has ruined us, he has taken all of what we own, and now wants to take our lives. In the first year, he despoiled us of the money we possessed; in the second year, he forced us to sell our lands, and in the third, we had to leave our homes because of the misery which has befallen us.'

I said to him, 'You lie! I have appointed as your governor a most virtuous man full of admirable qualities, worthy of respect and confidence, and one who can be trusted with your lives and fortunes.'

The group's spokesman replied, 'O Commander of the Faithful, what you have said is right and true: and what I have said is wrong and false. But you are the successor of God on this earth, and you are entrusted with the welfare of the people. Is it right that you reserve exclusively for our benefit this just, trusted and virtuous man? Isn't your duty to appoint him to govern other regions of the kingdom, so that he could spread his justice over the land, and extend to your other subjects the blessings of his rule which he has generously bestowed on us until now?'

I laughed and told the people, 'You can return to your homes, I have dismissed your governor.'

The second embarrassing situation in which I found myself happened when I visited the mother of al-Fadl.[109] She was inconsolable and wept continually over the loss of her son. I wanted to comfort her and I said to her, 'Why do you grieve and weep over your son's death, I will be a son for you in his stead!'

Instead of comforting her, my words seemed to increase her grief, and she said to me in a voice broken by tears, 'O Commander of the Faithful, how shall I not grieve over a son who made me gain a son like you?'

I could not find a word to say to her in reply and left.[110]

THE STORY OF FEYROUZ

It is said that a king one day went up on the roof of his palace to bask in the sunshine and saw on the roof of a neighbouring house a young woman of such rare beauty as he had never seen before. He asked a maidservant the name of the person who owned the neighbouring house. She replied, 'This house belongs to your servant Feyrouz, and the young woman on its roof is his wife.'

The king became enamoured of his beautiful neighbour, and conceived for her a violent passion. So one day he wrote a letter and sent for Feyrouz. When Feyrouz came, he handed him the letter and said to him, 'Take this letter tomorrow to my governor in such and such a town, and bring me his answer.' Feyrouz took the letter and

went home. He placed the letter under his pillow, and went to sleep. In the morning, he bade goodbye to his wife, and left on the king's errand.

No sooner had Feyrouz left, than the king hurried, in disguise, to the neighbouring house, and knocked on the door. The wife of Feyrouz asked, 'Who is at the door?'

The king replied, 'I am the king, and the master of your husband.'

Thereupon she opened the door and he entered. He took off his shoes in accordance with custom, and sat down. He then said to her, 'I have come to pay you a visit.'

The wife said: 'May God preserve me from the evil of such visit. I do not think there is any good in it!'

The king said, 'O desire of the hearts, I do not think you have recognized me!'

The wife said, 'Oh yes, I have recognized my lord and master, and I can guess what he is after. But my lord should remember the words of an ancient poet:

> I shall leave your water alone
> without drinking from it,
> Because of the number
> of those who come to it,
> If the flies fall on food,
> I pull back my hand even though my hunger is great,
> And the lions shun drinking from water
> if the dogs have lapped in it.

The king felt ashamed at what he heard, and went away. Overcome with emotion he forgot his shoes and left them behind.

As for Feyrouz, after he had walked part of the way, he realized that he had forgotten the king's letter, which remained under his pillow, and he returned to his home to fetch it. It happened that his return coincided with the king's leaving his house. On entering his home, he found the king's shoes. Feyrouz was furious when he realized that the king had despatched him on a mission only in furtherance of his evil design. But he kept silent, and said nothing. He took the king's letter, and departed on his mission. On his return, the king gave him one hundred dinars.

Feyrouz went to the souq, and with the money the king had given him he bought beautiful gifts suitable for women. He then went home, presented the gifts to his wife and said to her, 'Go now to your mother's house.'

She asked, 'What for?' and he replied, 'The king has favoured me with his kindness and I want your mother to enjoy the pleasure of seeing you wearing the presents I bought for you.'

The wife went to her mother's house and remained there for one whole month, without her husband coming to see her or to take her back. This seemed unusual, and worried the wife's brother, who suspected that something was amiss. So he went to Feyrouz, and said to him, 'You have sent back to us my sister and you have not informed us of the reason for your anger against her. Let us go to the king and ask him to judge between us.' Feyrouz accepted his suggestion and they both went to the king.

When they were admitted into the king's presence, they found the chief judge of the kingdom sitting with the king. The wife's brother said that he had a complaint to make against Feyrouz and the king ordered him to state it to the chief judge.

The wife's brother said to the judge, 'I have let to this young man a garden with high walls, a good well and trees laden with fruit. But he has pulled down its walls, destroyed the well, and now wants to return the garden to me.'

The judge turned to Feyrouz, and asked him, 'What do you say, young man?'

Feyrouz replied, 'I have returned the garden to him in better condition than when I took it from him.'

The judge asked the wife's brother, 'Has he returned to you the garden in the condition which he describes?'

The wife's brother said, 'No, but I want to know the reason for his returning the garden.'

The judge asked Feyrouz, 'Why did you return the garden?'

Feyrouz answered, 'I have returned the garden with reluctance. I have done so because I entered it one day, and found in it the trace of a lion. I am afraid if I enter it a second time that I shall be devoured by the lion. What I have done was out of fear and consideration for him!'

At these words, the king, who had been reclining on his pillow, sat up and said to Feyrouz, 'Return to your garden with your mind completely at rest. By God, I have never seen a garden like yours with its walls so secure and its trees so well protected.'

At these words, Feyrouz realized that his fears and doubts were unjustified and he took back his wife and they lived happily thereafter. Neither the judge, nor those who attended the king's court, ever realized the real implications of the story.[111]

HE WENT TO THE RIGHT DOCTOR

A man had pain in his eyes, and went to a vet for treatment. The vet put into his eyes the same medicine he used in treating animals. The patient instantly became blind. The case was brought before the qadi, who ruled that no offence had been committed and no compensation was recoverable, for had not the patient been an ass he would not have sought treatment with a vet![112]

DOUBLY STUPID

While waiting at the mill for his turn to have his wheat ground, a man took several handfuls of grain from his neighbour's bag, and put them into his own. The miller noticed the man's action, and said to him, 'What are you doing there?'

As an excuse the thief said, 'I am stupid!'

The miller said to him, 'If you are stupid, why don't you take wheat from your own bag and put it in your neighbour's bag?'

'If I were to do this,' replied the thief, 'I would be doubly stupid!'[113]

THE FAT KING'S HOROSCOPE

There was once a king who became so obese that he could hardly walk, or attend to his functions. The most eminent doctors of his kingdom were unable to find any remedy to reduce his weight or diminish his physical proportions. Every treatment they attempted only increased his corpulence.

Learning of the king's predicament, a man came to him and offered to treat his condition. The king told him, 'Cure me of my corpulence, and I shall make you a rich man.'

The man said to the king, 'You should be patient. I am both a doctor and an astrologer. Tonight I must first look into your horoscope to discover what remedy will suit you best.'

On the following day, the astrologer returned and said to the king, 'Do you want me to tell Your Majesty the truth, however painful it might be for you to hear it?'

The king insisted. 'You must tell me the truth.'

'I have examined your horoscope,' said the astrologer, 'and unfortunately I have found that you have only one more month to live. In these circumstances, your treatment would seem to have no object. If Your Majesty does not believe me, you can detain me in prison, and punish me if I am proved to be wrong.'

The king was alarmed and distressed by this news. He had the astrologer put in prison, and ordered the cessation of all festivities and public amusements. He isolated himself from the whole world, retiring into himself, and awaiting with grief and distress his approaching end. Each day that passed increased his despair. He completely lost his appetite, partook of no food and became thin and emaciated.

When the month elapsed and the king found himself still alive, he ordered that the astrologer be taken out of prison and brought before him. When the astrologer came, the king said to him, 'As you can see I have lost all my corpulence and I have returned to my normal size and weight. But do you still believe that I shall die as you predicted?'

The astrologer replied, 'Sire, may God give you a long life! Do you really believe there was any truth in my prediction? Your Majesty should realize that no one can predict the future which only God knows. I do not know myself how long I shall live. How then could I know how long you will live? But I had no remedy for your condition, except grief and distress which would make you lose your excess weight, and I could not cause you grief and distress except by making you believe that your end was near. I can see from your appearance that this treatment has fully succeeded!'

The king, having been rid both of his corpulence and of the fear of an impending death, was overjoyed and rewarded the astrologer liberally.[114]

A JUDGEMENT OF QARAQOASH

The expression 'a judgement of Qaraqoash' has among the Arabs come to mean a decision which is arbitrary, stupid and laughable. Qaraqoash was not an imaginary figure; he was one of Saladin's military commanders and lived in Cairo in the twelfth century. Although his existence is not legendary, the traits and actions popularly attributed to him are probably too laughable to possess any degree of authenticity. His comical reputation originated with a lampoon about him published by one of his contemporaries, a certain As'ad Ibn Mamati, also an army official at the time of Saladin. In this lampoon, entitled *Al-Fashoush fi Huqm Qaraqoash* the author tells a number of humorous anecdotes held up to ridicule Qaraqoash. Here is one of them:

There was in Cairo a merchant who was rich but avaricious. This miserly merchant had a son who was a spendthrift. The son borrowed from others in expectation of his father's early demise and on the strength of his future inheritance. But the old man continued to live, to the despair of his son and his son's creditors.

As the son's debts accumulated, and his creditors became more pressing and more impatient, the son and his creditors devised a

scheme to bury the father alive, open his succession, and distribute his estate. So one day they announced the old man's death and, despite his protests, laid him in a coffin and carried him to the cemetery. During the procession, their cries and shouts drowned out the man's protests.

It happened that Qaraqoash, the ruler of the city, was passing by and, out of courtesy, joined the funeral procession. When the supposedly dead man realized that Qaraqoash was present, he thought, 'Thank God, I am saved.' He sat up in his coffin and complained to Qaraqoash that his son wanted to bury him alive. Qaraqoash stopped the procession and, turning to the son, said to him, 'How dare you bury your father alive?' The son denied that his father was alive, 'When we put him in the coffin' he declared, 'he was dead, and all the people present here will testify to the truth of what I say.' Qaraqoash asked the people present – and they were all the son's creditors – whether they supported the son's story. As they were all in the conspiracy, they confirmed the truth of what the son had said.

Thereupon, Qaraqoash turned to the man in the coffin and said to him, 'Do you think I am crazy to believe you, and disbelieve all those here present?' And then he told the people to take the man and bury him.[115]

THE VILLAGE BARBER

The incident which I am about to narrate happened to me when I was in the country some years ago, before progress had yet reached Egyptian villages. I can blame only myself for what occurred, because my host had offered me the use of his razor, but I refused it, saying that so long as there was a barber in the village, then I wanted him to come and shave my beard.[116] My host warned me, cautioned me, and

lectured me, but all without success as I insisted that the barber should come to shave me.

After a few hours the barber came, carrying with him a large pair of scissors, and what at first I thought to be a nose-bag containing barley for animal feed. He greeted me, sat down and started to converse with me, which made me think that I was perhaps mistaken, and that he was someone else who might have been sent on a reconnaissance mission. When I grew impatient with his conversation, I asked him about the village barber. He stroked his beard with his hand and said to me, 'I am your man!'

I cursed him mentally, and asked him if he proposed to shave my beard or whether he thought it necessary to draw lines in the sand beforehand so as to determine the most propitious time at which he should begin the operation. As he did not seem to understand what I meant, I began shouting at him, and this appeared to amuse him greatly.

I then asked him whether there were any elephants in the village? He replied, 'Elephants? What for?'

I pointed to the large scissors he had brought with him and which seemed designed for the shearing of elephants. At this he laughed heartily and said, 'Excuse me, but those are donkey scissors!'

I said, 'You come to me with donkey scissors. Do you happen to take me for one?' It seemed to me, however, that living among donkeys had dulled his intelligence, and he did not apologize to me, or pay any attention to my remark.

He then pulled out from the nose-bag a large razor and a huge hair clipper. I was amazed that he had brought with him all these implements eminently suited for animals, and I asked him the reason.

He replied, 'God is with those who patiently persevere,'[117] and he invited me to squat down on the floor.

I asked, 'What for?', and he replied, 'Don't you want to be shaved?'
I objected. 'But can't you shave me while I am sitting in the chair?'
He replied, 'What about me?'

In the face of this logic, I had no choice but to squat down on the floor as he had ordered me to do.

He then opened the razor, which to me looked more like a metal file. I told him, 'Be careful, my face is not made of metal!'

He replied, 'By the grace of God, don't be afraid,' but by the grace of God I was afraid. He started the operation by saying, 'In the name of God,' as if I were a sheep that he wanted to sacrifice. He then spat into the palm of his hand, sharpened his razor on it, and jerked my head towards him. I was so terrified that I leapt and ran to the far corner of the room.

'What do you think you are doing?' he shouted.

'Do you want to shave me with a metal file, and without any soap?' I shouted back.

'What are you frightened of?' he asked, quite amazed at my behaviour.

'I am frightened', I replied, 'because I asked you to shave my beard, not to file it with a metal file!'

He said: '*Ya effendi*, don't be afraid.'

He then recited a verse from the Holy Qur'an: 'When fear had passed from the mind of Abraham, and the glad tidings had reached him . . .' until the end of the verse.[118] I thought to myself what kind of beard-shaving was this if it could be carried out only with the help of incantations. But I put my fate in the hands of God, and returned and sat on the floor in front of him. Thereupon, he seized my head with his two hands, turned my face towards him, put his knees on my thigh, and passed his arm around my neck so that my mouth was buried in his breast. I shrieked, or, more exactly, I tried to shriek, in the hope that someone might hear me and come to my rescue. But the folds of his garment were in my mouth, and the odour of his clothes made me lose consciousness. So as not to tire the reader, I shall not prolong the narration of what followed, but I shall tell how he swooped down on my face with his razor, started to skin me and actually stripped a piece of skin from my cheek. The pain made me recover consciousness, and I jumped up and made a dash for the door. But despite his advanced years, he was quicker than I was. How do I know, maybe he had anticipated what I would do, and experience had taught him to beware of similar escape attempts by his victims. So he seized me, pushed me back inside the room, and forced me to submit to the rest of the operation.

I felt like a martyr and recalled in my mind the verse of al-Mutanabbi:[119]

If from death there is found no escape,
One should not as a coward die.

He then brought a basin, which was so large that a ram could have drowned in it, and placed it under my chin. He poured a substance over my face, my breast, and my back to wash away my precious blood which he had spilt. He then pulled out from his nose-bag what was supposedly a towel, but which looked more like a floor mop. However, I gave him no time to perpetrate this new foul act. I politely asked him to excuse me, seized my handkerchief and wiped my face before he could mop it up with his floor rag, and ran away.[120]

THE DISADVANTAGE OF HAVING TWO WIVES

A man had two wives, one young, the other older.

The young wife disliked the white hairs that grew in her husband's beard, because it made him look older. So each time he came to see her, she plucked out the white hairs of his beard.

The older wife disliked the black hairs remaining in her husband's beard for fear that he might think himself younger than he was and marry again. So each time he came to see her, she plucked out the black hairs in his beard.

As a result of the combined efforts of those two ladies, the poor man lost both the white hairs and the black hairs of his beard, and eventually was left without any beard at all; a condition which reduces one's dignity and manliness among the Arabs.

When asked what had happened to his beard, he would say, 'Between my two wives, I lost my beard!' and this became a proverb among the Arabs.[121]

THE USE OF THE TURBAN

An Egyptian peasant happened to be in Cairo when he received a letter from his family in the provinces. As he was illiterate, he started looking around for someone to read it to him. His choice fell upon a sheikh passing by in the street, who was wearing a large and imposing turban,[122] which of course, is a sign of profound learning. He hurried to the sheikh and asked him if he would read the letter to him. The sheikh examined the letter carefully, but it was so badly scribbled that he was completely unable to decipher a single word of it. Regretfully,

he gave back the letter to the peasant and told him it was illegible, and that he was unable to read it.

This enraged the peasant.

'You are unable to read this letter?' he shouted at the sheikh, 'of what use then is your turban?'

Irritated by this remark, the sheikh removed his turban, stuck it on the head of the peasant, and said to him, 'Now you read it!'[123]

THE ESSENCE OF COMPLAINT

A husband had a violent quarrel with his wife, and as a result he threatened to repudiate her. They had been married for a long time, and when the wife realized that her husband was deadly serious in his threat, she sought to dissuade him by reminding him of their long married life.

'Think,' she told him, 'of the many years I have spent with you!'

'That's exactly my complaint!' retorted the husband ironically.[124]

HE INSISTED ON RECITING HIS POEM

Hafez Ibrahim, one of Egypt's modern poets, possessed a rare sense of humour. He was asked to deliver at the cemetery the eulogy of a deceased politician, and a large crowd of people attended the ceremony, including a number of poets. Among those present was a poet from the country, who came to the ceremony riding on his donkey.

Hafez began to deliver his eulogy in verse, but in the middle of it he was interrupted by the donkey with its loud and interminable braying. Thereupon, Hafez stopped and said to the crowd, 'We have to wait until our colleague's donkey has finished reciting his poem.'[125]

ONE GOOD REASON

It is said that the sultan of Turkey made an official visit to the city of Acre at the turn of the century. The governor of the city, the officials and notables all turned out to welcome him, but, contrary to custom, no guns were fired to salute his arrival. This greatly offended the sultan who gave an order for the immediate beheading of the governor. The latter, trembling with fear, protested to the sultan that there were a hundred reasons to explain why no guns had been fired on his arrival. The sultan dryly inquired what were those one hundred reasons. The governor said, 'Your Majesty, the first reason is that we have no guns. The second reason is . . .'

Here the sultan interrupted him and said, 'As your first reason is good, never mind about the ninety-nine others! You are pardoned!'[126]

HOW HE WON THE OFFICE OF GRAND VIZIER

A king wanted to appoint a grand vizier. Three candidates competed for the king's nomination to this high office, but the king was unable to decide which was the most intelligent and the most suitable for the post. At last, he decided to subject them to a competition, the winner of which would be chosen as grand vizier.

The king summoned the three candidates, and told them that he

had prepared five balls, three of which were white and two were black. He said he would place one ball on the turban of each of the three men. Each of them would be able to see the balls on the heads of the other two, but would have to guess the colour of the ball placed on his own head. The first one of them to make the correct guess would be appointed grand vizier.

The king then placed one ball on the turban of each of the candidates, and asked each in turn to guess the colour of the ball placed on his head. Two of the men were unable to make any guess at all, and remained silent. The third man said, 'I have a white ball on my head.'

He had guessed correctly, and the king asked him to explain how he was able to make a correct answer. The successful candidate explained that he first discarded the hypothesis that the king would place two black balls on the heads of two of the candidates, because on seeing them, the third man would immediately guess that he had a white ball on his head. Next he eliminated the possibility that the king would place a black ball on the head of one of the candidates. To arrive at this conclusion he reasoned as follows: if the black ball were placed on the head of one of the three men, this would simplify the guesswork of the other two candidates who, seeing a black ball on the head of the first man, and discounting the hypothesis that the king would place two black balls on the heads of two of the candidates, would immediately conclude that they had white balls on their heads. With these two hypotheses being eliminated, it was evident, therefore, that the king could only have placed white balls on the heads of all three candidates.[127]

A GRAVE DIPLOMATIC PROBLEM

When Turkish power was at its height, the sultan of Turkey decided to visit one of the countries of Europe. The sultan informed his grand vizier of his project, but the latter was greatly concerned.

'Your Majesty's voyage,' he said, 'is almost sure to result in grave international complications.'

'Why is that?' inquired the sultan.

'Because of an ancient rule of our kingdom,' replied the grand vizier, 'that the soil on which a Turkish sultan treads legally falls under Turkish sovereignty. The application of this rule would lead to a serious diplomatic problem, and a territorial dispute, if not a war, with the country that Your Majesty intends to visit.'

'I have made up my mind to undertake this voyage,' said the sultan, 'and nothing will make me change my plans. You had better find a way for me to undertake this voyage without becoming involved in any international complications.'

The grand vizier decided to consult Sheikh al-Islam, the chief justice, on the problem. This esteemed and learned person said to the grand vizier, 'There is no question of changing or abrogating this ancient rule of our empire. The soil on which our master treads legally becomes Turkish territory. But the application of this rule could be avoided by an artifice. You should order special shoes to be made, which our sovereign can wear during his voyage abroad. These shoes must have double soles with an empty space between them to be filled with Turkish soil. When our sovereign treads on foreign land during his voyage abroad, he will, in fact, be treading on Turkish soil. This will prevent the legal acquisition by our country of a right of sovereignty over foreign lands which our sovereign has no ambition to acquire.'

Thanks to the artifice suggested by the chief justice, the sultan was able to undertake a voyage free from worries of political complications.[128]

THE HAUNTED CAVERN

The belief in ghosts and jinns is prevalent among the Arabs, particularly among the country people.

It happened that one evening the young men of a village in Palestine were telling each other stories about ghosts and jinns. The conversation turned upon a cavern in a nearby mountain which, according to local belief, was haunted by ghosts. One of the young men ridiculed the idea. Thereupon, the others dared him to go to the cavern at night. The young man took up the challenge, and said he would go to the cavern that very night. As proof of his feat, he was required to take with him a peg which he would drive into the floor of the cavern, and in the morning they would all go to inspect it.

The young man took the peg and went to the cavern. The night was pitch-black. When he reached the cavern he entered and, squatting down, he drove the peg deeply into the ground with a stone. He then rose to go, but was held back by something invisible. He tried to pull himself away with all his strength, but to no avail: he was, as it were, pegged to the ground.

The young man's companions were greatly concerned that he did not return to the village and in the early hours of the morning they hurried to look for him. They found him dead in the cavern beside the peg that he had driven into the floor. In the darkness, when he had squatted down to drive the peg into the ground, he had driven it through a fold in his robe and thus pegged himself to the floor of the cave. The courageous young man had died of fright.[129]

Notes

1   *Halbat al-Kumait*, p.11; *al-Mustatraf*, vol. I, p. 132; *Bada'e' al-Zuhur*, p. 73. It is interesting to observe that an English criminal writer, Kenny, has pointed out that there are three stages in drunkenness: the jocose, the bellicose and the comatose.

2   Al-Hajjaj (AD 661–714) was governor of the Umayyads in Iraq.

3   *Al-Mustatraf*, vol. I, p. 59.

4   A famous Persian king.

5   *Al-Basa'er wal-Zhakha'er*, vol. IV, p. 26; *al-Mustatraf*, vol. I, p. 104.

6   *Al-Mustatraf*, vol. I, p. 145; *Thamarat al-Awraq*, p. 167; *al-Azkiya'*, p. 42.

7   Abu Hanifa (AD 699–767), a theologian and religious lawyer, was a foremost authority in his time on questions of religious law in Kufa in Iraq.

8   *Al-Mustatraf*, vol. I, p. 146; al-Midani, *Majma' al-Amthal*, vol. I, p. 338.

9   *Al-Mustatraf*, vol. I, p. 195; *al-Majani al-Haditha*, vol. V, p. 107.

10   *Al-Mustatraf*, vol. II, p. 10.

11   *Nawader al-Qaliobi*, p. 51; *al-Mustatraf*, vol. II, p. 119; *Nuzhat al-Jalees*, vol. II, p. 62. A detailed version of this anecdote is found in A. J. Arberry, *Tales from the Masnavi*, p. 68, George Allen and Unwin, London.

12   Al-Jahez, *al-Hayawan*, vol. II, p. 130; *Nihayat al-Arab*, vol. I, p. 17; *Nawader al-Qaliobi*, p. 163.

13   Haroun al-Rashid (AD 766–809), one of the most famous Abbasid Caliphs.

14   *Al-Mustatraf*, vol. II, p. 275.

15   Al-Jahez (AD 775–868), a famous Arab writer of the ninth century.

16   *Al-Hayawan*, vol. V, p. 539.

17   *Majani al-Adab*, vol. II, p. 171.

18   Siavash-Danesh, *An Anthology of Persian Prose*, p. 95, Vahid Publishing Company, Teheran, 1971.

19   Mohamed Ben Abdallah al-Mahdi (AD 744–785), Abbasid caliph.

20   *Thail Zahr al-Adab*, p. 101; *al-Mustatraf*, vol. II, p. 296.

21   Khaled Ibn Safwan, man of literature, died AD 750.

22   Al-Saffah (AD 722–754), Abbasid caliph.

23   Muslim law 'undoubtedly contemplates monogamy as the ideal to be aimed at, but concedes to a man the right to have more than one wife, not exceeding four, at one and the same time, provided he is able to deal with them on a footing of equality and justice': Abdur Rahim, *Muhammadan Jurisprudence*, p. 327, Luzac & Co., 1911.

24   *Nafhat al-Yumn*, p. 136.

25   Died in AD 840.

26   *Majani al-Adab*, vol. I, p. 62.

27 *Fakihat al-Khulafa'*, p. 161.

28 *Thail Zahr al-Adab*, p. 123.

29 In Arab countries the snake charmer (*hawi*) is called in to kill snakes that take up residence in homes.

30 *Al-Hayawan*, vol. V, p. 256.

31 *Al-Hayawan*, vol. IV, p. 459.

32 Based upon an anecdote of Nizami, *Makhzanul Asrar*, cited in Edward G. Browne's *Arabian Medicine*, and its French translation, *La Médecine Arabe*, H. P. Renaud, p. 100, Paris.

33 *Majani al-Adab*, vol. I, p. 94; *al-Mustatraf*, vol. II, p. 243; *Nafhat al-Yumn*, p. 87.

34 *Majani al-Adab*, vol. I, p. 64; *Fakihat al-Khulafa'*, p. 51.

35 Bar-Hebraeus, *Laughable Stories*, edited and translated from the Syriac by E. A. Wallis Budge, p. 85, Luzac and Co., London 1897.

36 *Thail Zahr al-Adab*, p. 280.

37 *Al-Hayawan*, vol. V, p. 228.

38 Al Ma'moun (AD 786–833), Abbasid caliph, son of Haroun al-Rashid.

39 *Hadiqat al-Afrah*, p. 37.

40 Sheikh Ibn Abi Laylah (AD 693–765), chief justice of Kufa in Iraq. The metamorphosis of human beings, jinns or animals is fairly common in oriental tales and anecdotes.

41 *Thail Zahr al-Adab*, p. 187; *Al-'Iqd al-Fareed*, vol. IV, p. 383, *Nuzhat al-Jalees*, vol. II, p. 35.

42 *Muhadarat al-Udaba'*, vol. IV, p. 707.

43 This anecdote is reproduced from *Persian Proverbs* by L. P. Elwell-Sutton, p. 42, John Murray, London, 1954.

44 Translated from R. Basset, *Contes Arabes*, vol. I, p. 516.

45 Abu Nouwas (AD 763–814), poet of Iraq.

46 Mgr. Michel Feghali, *Proverbes et dictons Syro-Libanais*, p. 23.

47 *Majma' al-Amthal*, vol. I, p. 105.

48 Bar-Hebraeus, *Laughable Stories*, translated by E. A. Wallis Budge, p. 91, Luzac and Co., London 1897.

49 The narrator of tradition is called the *muhaddeth* and he narrates the *hadith* or the sayings of the Prophet. To be accepted as authentic, the *hadith* must be based upon reliable and trustworthy sources or on a chain of authorities.

50 *Thamarat al-Awraq*, p. 55; *al-Mustatraf*, vol. II, p. 262; *Halbat al-Kumait*, p. 17.

51 Bar-Hebraeus, *Laughable Stories*, translated by E. A. Wallis Budge, p. 112, Luzac & Co., London 1897.

52 A coin worth a small sum.

53 Bar-Hebraeus, *Laughable Stories*, translated by E. A. Wallis Budge, p. 123, Luzac and Co., London, 1897.

54 *Hadith* are the words and deeds of the Prophet, which are accepted as Islamic tradition.

55 'Uyun al-Akhbar, vol. IV, p. 55; al-'Iqd al-Fareed, vol. IV, p. 375.
56 Al-Azkiya', p. 87.
57 Al-Azkiya', p. 145.
58 This anecdote is reproduced from Persian Proverbs, by L. P. Elwell-Sutton, p. 43, John Murray, London, 1954.
59 Al-Fakihat fil-Adab, p. 49; al-'Iqd al-Fareed, vol. III, p. 332.
60 Nafhat al-Yumn, p. 87.
61 Bar-Hebraeus, Laughable Stories, edited and translated by E. A. Wallis Budge, p. 157, Luzac and Co., London, 1897.
62 Siavash-Danesh, An Anthology of Persian Prose, p. 112, Vahid Publishing Company, Teheran, 1971.
63 Al-Mustatraf, vol. 1, p. 20; al-Basa'er wal Zhakha'er, p. 84.
64 The dinar was a gold coin.
65 The dirhem was a silver coin that had the value of one-tenth of a dinar.
66 Hadiqat al-Afrah, p. 146.
67 Al-Mansour (AD 714–775), Abbassid Caliph.
68 Nihayat ai-Arab, vol. IV, p. 117.
69 Among the bedouins, the slaughter of a camel for a guest is considered to be the greatest honour done to him. Next in importance is the slaughter of a sheep and the last in the scale of hospitality is the slaughter of a chicken.
70 Al-Mustatraf, vol. I, p. 20; al-Basa'er wal-Zhakha'er, p. 84.
71 This is the usual phrase used in Arab countries to send away a beggar without giving him any alms.
72 Nihayat al-Arab, vol. IV, p. 23.
73 Al-Imta' wal-Mu'anasa, vol. III, p.28.
74 The Life and Works of Jahez edited by Charles Pellat, p.241, Routledge and Kegan Paul, and University of California Press.
75 Al-Asma'i (AD 740–831), famous narrator of tradition, poetry and literature.
76 Halbat al-Kumait, p. 71.
77 Al-Basa'er wal-Zhakha'er, p. 87.
78 Majani al-Adab, vol. I, p. 97.
79 Al-Basa'er wal-Zhakha'er, vol. II, p. 727.
80 Siavash-Danesh, An Anthology of Persian Prose, p. 98, Vahid Publishing Company, Teheran, 1971.
81 Nafhat al-Yumn, p. 7.
82 Imam Shafe'i was a tenth-century legal scholar who lived and taught in Iraq and Egypt. His writings form one of the foundations of Islamic jurisprudence. Imam means an Islamic religious leader.
83 It is a custom of Muslims to take off their shoes when they enter a mosque, or when they are at prayers.
84 Translated from R. Basset, Contes Arabes, vol. I, p. 334; Nuzhat al-Udaba', p. 52.
85 Al-'Iqd al-Fareed, vol. IV, p. 221.

86   L. P. Elwell-Sutton, *Persian Proverbs*, p. 73, John Murray, London, 1954.

87   Based on a story by al-Nawaji, *Halbat al-Kumait*, p. 56.

88   *Al-'Iqd al-Fareed*, Vol. IV, p. 382.

89   Under Islamic law, interdiction is an order of the judge which deprives a person of his right to deal with his property by reason of his wastefulness or weakness of mind, which makes him unable to manage his own affairs.

90   Translated from R. Basset, *Contes Arabes*, vol. II, p. 321.

91   *Nafhat al-Yumn*, p. 162.

92   Bar-Hebraeus, *Laughable Stories*, p. 90.

93   Al-Sha'bi (AD 640–721), narrator of tradition, judge and poet.

94   Abdul Malek Ibn Mirwan (AD 646–705), Umayyad caliph.

95   *Nafhat al-Yumn*, p. 91.

96   *Nuzhat al-Jalees*, vol. I, p. 374.

97   *Muhhadarat al-Udaba'*, vol. II, p. 588; *Jawaher al-Adab*, vol. I., p. 414.

98   This is the usual exchange of greetings between Arabs.

99   *Muhadarat al-Udaba'*, vol. III, p. 191.

100 *Hadiqat al-Afrah*, p. 36.

101 *Akhbar al-Hamqa*, p. 65.

102 Under Islamic procedure, if a plaintiff has no proof in support of his claim, he can demand the defendant's oath concerning the truth of his action. If the defendant refuses to take the oath, the judge will give judgment against him. If, however, he accepts to take the oath, and swears that he owes nothing to the plaintiff, the judge will dismiss the plaintiff's action.

103 *Akhbar al-Hamqa*, p. 65.

104 *Thail Zahr al-Adab*, p. 149; *'Uyun al-Akhbar*, vol. III, p. 263.

105 In accordance with Islamic belief, the Angel of Death is charged by Allah with fetching a man's soul at the time of his death.

106 Based on an anecdote of Kamaliddin Halaby in *Majani al-Adab*, vol. II, p. 203. A Persian version of this anecdote is found in *Tales from the Masnavi* by A. H. Arberry, p. 75, George Allen and Unwin, London, and in *Persian Folktales*, G. Bell and Sons, p. 122.

107 *Al-Mustatraf*, vol. I, p. 10.

108 *Hadiqat al-Afrah*, p. 147.

109 Al-Fadl (AD 711–818) was an influential minister of al-Ma'moun and was renowned for his wisdom. He was assassinated in his bath.

110 *Hadiqat al-Afrah*, p. 128.

111 *Hadiqat al-Afrah*, p. 144; *al-Mustatraf*, vol. II, p. 204.

112 A story of Saadi of Shiraz from *An Anthology of Persian Prose* by Siavash-Danesh, p. 92, Vahid Publishing Company, Teheran, 1971.

113 *Alef Ba'*, vol. I, p. 536; *Akhbar Juha*, p. 114.

114 *Thamarat al-Awraq*, p. 86; *Nafhat al-Yumn*, p. 173.

115 *Al-Fashoush fi Huqm Qaraqoash*, p. 25.

116 In times gone by, in some places in the Middle East the barber was sometimes called to shave a client at home.

117 The Qur'an, s.2, v. 153.
118 The Qur'an, s.11, v. 74.
119 Al-Mutanabbi (AD 915–965), a famous Arab poet.
120 This anecdote is narrated by Ibrahim Abdel Qader al-Mazini, one of Egypt's modern writers, in *Soundouq al-Dunia*, p. 76.
121 *Bain hana wa mana da'at Ilhana*. This proverb is used to explain the failure of a scheme or undertaking as a result of the interference of the parties acting with conflicting aims.
122 The turban is the headgear of sheikhs, who are learned in the law.
123 *Al-Fashoush fi Huqm Qaraqoash*, p. 142.
124 *Nafhat al-Yumn*, p. 69.
125 *Kitab al-Uns*, p. 497.
126 This story is anonymous and was heard by the author in Palestine.
127 This story is anonymous and was heard by the author in Palestine.
128 The subterfuge described in this anecdote found an improper application in an authentic case that came to the author's knowledge during his legal practice in Palestine. An unscrupulous plaintiff adopted it in order to establish his claim to a disputed plot of land. The Court had ordered an inspection of the land, and decided to hear the evidence of the witnesses on the spot. So the crafty plaintiff supplied his witnesses with shoes that had double soles, between which he placed some earth taken from another plot of land that he did actually own. On the day of the court's inspection of the disputed property, the plaintiff's witnesses, wearing their double-soled shoes, swore that the soil (between their soles) on which they stood belonged to the plaintiff.
129 This story is anonymous and was heard by the author in Palestine.

PART II

STORIES OF JUHA

JUHA GIVES JUDGEMENT

An old beggar knocked on the door of a house and asked for charity. He was given a piece of dry bread which his teeth could not bite into. He put the piece of bread in his bag and went away. As he walked through the souq, he passed a cook's shop, and saw at its entrance a large pot boiling over a fire. The pot steamed and emitted a delicious smell of spicy food. It occurred to the beggar that if he were to hold his dry bread over the boiling pot and moisten it in the vapour, the bread would be softened, and he would then be able to eat it. This he did, to the surprise of the cook who watched the strange operation.

When the bread was moistened, the beggar ate it. As he was about to leave, the cook came to him and demanded payment. The beggar objected that he had not eaten any of the cook's food, since all he had done was to moisten his bread in the vapour that steamed out from the pot. The cook insisted on being paid compensation for this, and as he did not get satisfaction he dragged the beggar to Juha, who was then the judge of the town.

Juha heard the cook's complaint and the beggar's defence, and by way of judgement, he drew a few coins from his pocket, clinked them vigorously in the palm of his hand, and then, addressing himself to the cook, said, 'Do you hear this clinking of coins? It is the compensation due to you. Whoever sells the vapour of food receives the clinking of coins in remuneration.'

THE BULL KNOWS THE REASON

A neighbour's bull broke down Juha's garden fence, and devoured his bed of lettuce. When Juha saw the damage done by the bull, he seized a thick stick, ran after the animal, and began beating it furiously. His neighbour, who saw him, shouted at him, 'What are you doing there, Juha?'

'Don't you interfere in this matter, which is strictly between me and your bull,' replied Juha angrily, without stopping his punishment of the animal.

'But for what reason are you beating my bull?' cried the neighbour.

'Never mind the reason,' exclaimed Juha, 'your bull knows why he is being beaten.'

INSIDE OR OUT?

Juha had a sheepskin coat which he used to wear inside out, that is, with the wool on the outside, contrary to the usual custom of wearing such coats. When people asked him why he did so, he would reply, 'In this matter I follow the divine way. If God, in His Wisdom, had thought it better that the wool should be worn on the inside, He would not have created the sheep with its wool on the outside.'

JUHA TRADES IN EGGS

One day Juha thought he would set up in business, and decided to trade in eggs. So he opened a shop, bought a consignment of eggs, and started selling them. His principal concern, however, was to buy and sell and to show a considerable activity, regardless of whether he made any profit or not. Since most of the time he sold his eggs cheaper than he bought them, he soon lost both his capital and his eggs, and became bankrupt. The expression 'Like Juha's trading in eggs' has since become a popular Arab saying, used to describe a commercial venture that fails by reason of the incompetence or the inexperience of the person undertaking it.

WHO IS TO BE BELIEVED?

A neighbour came to Juha and said, 'Lend me your donkey, for suddenly I find I have to go on a journey.' Juha, who did not wish to lend the man his donkey, replied, 'I would willingly lend it to you, but alas, I sold it yesterday.'

Just then, the donkey which was in the stable began to bray in a deafening manner. The neighbour jumped. 'But your donkey is in the stable,' he remonstrated.

Juha replied angrily, 'You fool, would you take the word of an ass against mine?'

The neighbour did not know whom to believe, and went away.

THE PROPER TIME FOR MEALS

Juha was asked the question, 'What is the proper time for taking meals?' and he replied, 'It depends. For the man who has something to eat, the most convenient time to eat is when he feels hungry. But for the man who has nothing to eat, he does not have that choice: he eats when he finds food.'

A DIFFICULT CAT TO PLEASE

Juha sat down to eat. He had before him some bread and cheese. A cat came near to him and began mewing. Juha threw a piece of bread to the animal. The cat sniffed it, but did not eat it and continued to mew, even more insistently. Juha then threw to the cat a piece of cheese. Again the cat sniffed it and left it alone, mewing more loudly. Juha then pulled a small coin out of his pocket, threw it to the cat and said, 'Now you go along with this coin and buy yourself something that you really like to eat.'

NAME THE CHILD 'SWIFT'

A woman gave birth to a child six months after her marriage. As the husband was away, the women of the village gathered together to discuss what name to give to the baby. Having failed to agree on the name of the child they decided to consult Juha. They went to him, and asked him what name should be given to the newly-born child. Juha thought for a minute and said, 'The child should be called "Swift".'

The women of the village objected that never before had they heard of such a name. But Juha convincingly explained to them the reason for his choice of such a name: 'This name fits the child. One who can cover a distance of nine months in six, should be named "Swift".'

TAKE MY HAND

The miser of the village fell into a pond which had high banks around it. He did not know how to swim. He struggled desperately in the water, and cried for help. The bystanders on the bank shouted to him, 'Give us your hand!' But giving was not a trait of his nature, and so he instinctively held back his hand, and the people could not reach him to pull him out of the water.

He was about to drown, when Juha who had watched the scene shouted to the people who were trying to save him, 'Get back. You don't know how to talk to this man. He is not used to giving, but only to taking.'

Juha then bent forward and shouted to the miser, 'Bakr *effendi*,[1] take my hand, take my hand!' The drowning man said, 'God bless you, my son,' and immediately he grabbed Juha's hand and was pulled ashore to safety.

JUHA GRIEVES OVER HIS DONKEY

Juha's wife died but strangely enough he did not show signs of a deep sorrow. Some time later his donkey died, he wept bitterly and showed great grief. He appeared to be more affected by the loss of his donkey than by the death of his wife. As someone reproached him for his attitude in this regard, Juha said in explanation, 'When my wife died, my friends and neighbours all came and consoled me. They begged me not to feel afflicted, and they assured me that they would find me another wife, even better than the deceased one. But when my donkey died, no one came to console me, nor to share my grief, and no one offered to find me another one to replace him.'

THE SAUCE OF THE SAUCE

A man from the country came to see Juha, and brought him a rabbit as a present. Juha thanked him and received him well.

A few days later, two visitors arrived at Juha's house and said to him, 'We are the neighbours of the man who brought you the rabbit.' Juha welcomed them and invited them to dinner.

A week later, four men arrived at Juha's house and told him that they were the neighbours of the neighbours of the man who had brought him the rabbit. They sat down, and it soon became obvious that they were expecting Juha to invite them to stay for dinner. Thereupon Juha went to the kitchen and fetched a large bowl filled with hot water. He placed the bowl before the visitors, handed a spoon to each of them, and told them, 'Help yourselves.'

When the visitors tasted what was in the bowl they expressed deep surprise, and asked Juha 'O virtuous sheikh, what kind of soup is this?'

Juha replied, 'O neighbours of the neighbours of the owner of the rabbit, this is the sauce of the sauce of the rabbit.'

WHOSE MISFORTUNE WAS THE GREATER?

Juha was a close companion of Tamerlane, who appreciated the sheikh's wisdom and enjoyed his sense of humour. One day Tamerlane wanted to review his troops and invited the sheikh to attend. The sheikh accepted the invitation and came to Tamerlane's tent. Tamerlane donned his ceremonial dress and, before leaving his tent, took a look at his face in a mirror. He was greatly saddened by the ugliness of his appearance. Turning to the sheikh, Tamerlane complained to him, 'When I look at my face in a mirror, I feel my misfortune.' To console him Juha told him, 'Your Excellency will pardon me if I say that my misfortune is greater. You have looked at your face once in the mirror and you have felt depressed. What about me who has to look at your face day after day?'

A DIVISION ACCORDING TO THE RULE OF GOD

A wealthy man of the village died, leaving four sons. Juha was asked by his heirs to divide the estate between them. He agreed to make the division and asked them, 'Do you want a division in accordance with the rule of God, or a man-made division?' They all said they wanted a division according to the rule of God.

Accordingly, Juha divided the state as follows: he gave one of the sons two dinars, to another fifteen thousand dinars, to the third an old mattress, and to the last one twelve cows and three sheep. The heirs vigorously protested and asked Juha, 'Is this a division according to the rule of God?'

Juha replied, 'Surely it is, just look around you, and you can see the differences between the fortunes that God bestows upon men.'

THE SUN AND THE MOON

Juha was asked, 'Which is more useful, the sun or the moon?'

Unhesitatingly, Juha replied, 'The moon, no doubt.'

Asked to explain the reason, he said, 'Well, it is like this. The sun rises during the day when people have no need for it, whereas the moon rises in the dark when people are in great need of it.'

THE ETHICS OF WALKING IN A FUNERAL PROCESSION

A simpleton inquired of Juha the ethics of walking in a funeral procession: 'What is better, to walk behind or in front of the coffin?'

Juha replied, 'Provided you are not yourself in the coffin, you may walk as you please.'

A DANGEROUS BUSINESS

Juha found a woman weeping by the side of a grave in a cemetery. He asked her, 'Who is the dead man?'

The woman replied, 'My husband.'

Juha asked her, 'What did he do in life?'

The woman replied, 'He dug pits for the graves in this cemetery.'

Juha shook his head in disapproval and told the woman, 'Your husband brought this misfortune on his own head. Digging pits is a dangerous business. Didn't he know that the proverb says: whoever digs a pit will fall into it?'

WASTED EFFORTS

Some thieves broke into Juha's house by night, and began searching for something to steal. Juha woke up and watched their search with curiosity and amusement.

Seeing, however, that they persisted in their fruitless efforts, Juha said to them, 'O young men, do not waste your time and efforts. Whatever you are seeking to find in this house by night, I have looked for very carefully by day, but I have not found it.'[2]

JUHA'S PEG[3]

Juha wanted to sell his house, but he insisted on one condition: he wanted to retain the ownership of a peg in the hall of the house. The buyer thought that leaving to Juha the ownership of a peg in the house was not, and could not be, of great consequence, and so he agreed to the condition and the sale was concluded on that basis.

Early the following day, Juha came and knocked on the buyer's door and said he wanted to come in to hang something on the peg. He returned the next day, and took away what he had hung on the peg on the day before. The same thing happened each day, and sometimes several times a day. Juha was in and out of the house more often than its owner. What made things even worse was that on certain occasions he hung on the peg a parcel containing food, meat or fish which rotted, and its putrid smell made the house uninhabitable. Moreover, the buyer of the house could do nothing about it, for he was bound by Juha's condition.

In the end, the owner of the house realized that because of Juha's peg he could not live in peace in the house. He tried to find a buyer for the house, but no one would buy it on account of Juha's peg. Finally he was compelled to beg Juha to take back his house at a ridiculously low price which Juha professed to do with reluctance, and only to oblige the unfortunate owner.

THE PARROT AND THE TURKEY

One day, while Juha was at the animal market, he saw a parrot being sold there for twelve gold coins. He said to himself, 'Why don't I sell my turkey. He is larger in size and louder in voice. He should fetch a much higher price than this painted bird.'

On the following day, he carried his turkey under his arm to the market and offered it for sale. The highest bid made for the turkey was a paltry sum of twelve piastres. This irritated Juha considerably, and he did not mince his words in criticism of those who paid twelve gold coins for a painted bird, but who offered only twelve piastres for a big and beautiful turkey.

One of the spectators tried to explain to Juha the reason for the difference in the price of the two birds. He told him that the parrot that had been sold the day before was not painted; its colours were natural, and, moreover, the other bird could even speak. Incensed at this explanation, Juha retorted. 'The other may speak, this one *thinks!*'

WHO IS SELLING THE PICKLES?

Juha decided to become a street hawker and to sell pickles. He acquired a few jars of pickles, loaded them onto his donkey, and started out in the narrow streets of his town, crying 'Pickles, pickles.'

But each time he cried, 'Pickles, pickles', his donkey would bray deafeningly and make his voice inaudible. This irritated Juha so much that he shouted angrily at his donkey, 'Look here, who is selling the pickles, your or I?'

THE TIME FOR PUNISHMENT

Juha gave his young servant a jar to fill with water at the village well. As he gave him the jar, he slapped the boy's face and told him, 'Take care not to break the jar.' Whereupon, the boy burst into tears.

The people who saw Juha strike his servant reproached him for his action, and said to him, 'How can you beat your boy when he did no wrong?'

Juha replied, 'I wanted to show him what would be the punishment for breaking the jar so that he would take care not to break it. What is the point of punishing him after the jar is broken?'

TEACHING THE DONKEY

There was a sultan who had a pet white donkey of which he was very fond. However, it was a source of unhappiness to him that the donkey could not speak.

The sultan searched all over the country for someone who would undertake to teach his donkey to speak, but he could find no one willing to undertake this assignment. Then one day Juha, who had heard of this curious quest, went to the sultan and offered his services to him. He would teach his donkey to speak, he told the sultan, but he attached certain conditions; he needed ten years to teach the donkey to speak, and during this period he wanted a house, two servants, food for himself and fodder for the animal, so that he could devote himself exclusively to his work. The sultan accepted Juha's conditions. He gave Juha a house, servants and money, but warned him that he would be answerable in the event that he failed to fulfil his promise. According to the custom of the time, this meant that if he

did not fulfil his promise, he would be beheaded without mercy.

With his means of livelihood assured for several years to come, Juha led a happy and easy life. But as time went by, his friends came to him and said, 'Juha, you are a foolish idiot, you know very well that you cannot teach the donkey to speak, and you will surely be beheaded for failing to keep your promise to the sultan.'

But Juha reassured them, 'Why should I worry? During the ten years fixed in the bargain, one of three things might happen: the sultan may die, or I might die, or the donkey may die. Or, who knows, Allah is great and powerful, the donkey might perhaps learn to speak.'

A LUCKY ESCAPE

One day Juha lost his donkey. He looked for the animal everywhere but he could not find it. People were amazed to see that he was not saddened by his loss but, on the contrary, they heard him thank God from the bottom of his heart. They asked him, how was it that he thanked God for the loss of his donkey. Juha replied, 'I thank God for my lucky escape because, had I been riding my donkey at the time, I might have been lost too!'

IF THIS IS THE CAT, WHERE IS THE MEAT?

Juha sent his wife three pounds of meat to cook for their dinner. The meat arrived simultaneously with some of the wife's friends who came unexpectedly to visit her. Having nothing to offer to them, she cooked the meat and they ate it all.

When Juha returned home in the evening, his wife was frightened to tell him the truth. Instead she told him, with tears in her eyes, that at one moment when she had her back turned, the cat had eaten the meat. Juha looked at the cat and could not believe his ears nor his eyes. He seized the cat, and put it on the scales. It weighed exactly three pounds. He held up the cat in the air, and turning to his wife asked her, 'If this is the cat, where is the meat? And if this is the meat, then where is the cat?'

THE DONKEY WITHHOLDS ITS CONSENT

A neighbour came to Juha and asked him to lend him his donkey to go to the neighbouring town. Juha replied that he would have to consult the donkey to see whether it would agree, and he went off to the stable. A little later he came back, and said to his neighbour, 'I have consulted the donkey, but it does not agree. It says the last time you borrowed it you beat it, cursed it and cursed its owner too.'

JUHA AND THE THIEVES

Thieves entered Juha's house one night and started taking away whatever they could lay their hands upon. When the thieves left the house with their loot, Juha collected what little they had left behind and followed them. The thieves noticed that Juha had followed them and asked him what he wanted.

Juha said, 'You have left me nothing in my house, so I have come to live with you.'

The thieves laughed, and returned to him his belongings.

THE HEAD AT THE WINDOW

One day Juha went to see one of his debtors to ask for the repayment of a sum of money. The debtor was leaning on the windowsill of his house and watching the activities in the street outside, but when he caught sight of Juha he quickly withdrew inside. Juha knocked on the door and when the servant came he asked to see the master. The servant coolly told Juha that he regretted to inform him that his master was not at home and that his master would be extremely sorry to learn on his return that Juha had called upon him in his absence and had not found him.

'Very well,' observed Juha, 'but be sure to tell your master on his return that when he goes away from his house, he should make sure not to leave his head at the window.

JUHA'S OVEN

Juha's wife complained to him one day about having to carry her dough daily to the baker in order to bake their bread. All her friends, she said, had their own ovens built in their courtyards. So Juha built an oven of clay bricks.

The oven was barely finished when a neighbour came to see Juha, and he stopped and stared in amazement at the construction. He turned around it, examined it carefully, and shook his head in disapproval.

'What is wrong with my oven?' demanded Juha.

'It faces west,' observed the neighbour, with a tragic tone in his voice.

'And why should it not face west?' inquired Juha.

'Because of the wind,' said the neighbour, with some authority. 'With your oven facing west, the wind will blow into it and put out your fire before your bread is baked.'

Juha was greatly disappointed. All his labour in building the oven was wasted. But as he was determined to let his wife have her own way, he lost no time in tearing down the oven and building a new one.

When the new oven was completed, another neighbour chanced to come and visit Juha. The neighbour appeared dumbfounded at the sight of the construction.

'What have you built here?' asked the neighbour.

'An oven,' replied Juha. 'Is there anything wrong with it?' he asked perplexed.

'Don't you see what is wrong with it?' observed the neighbour. 'It faces east.'

'And why shouldn't it face east?' demanded Juha.

'Because you will never have enough draught to start a fire in an oven that faces east,' replied the neighbour with conviction.

Again Juha demolished the oven and built a new one. This time, however, he built it on a push-cart. When it was completed, his neighbours came and expressed surprise at this queer construction.

'Why have you built your oven on wheels?' they asked him.

'Because in this manner it can be turned to any geographical direction my neighbours want it to face', he replied with an ironical smile.

JUHA LIGHTENS THE LOAD

Juha went to the market and filled the donkey's saddle-bags with various things he had bought. He then placed the saddle-bags across his shoulders, mounted on his donkey and returned home. On the way he met one of his friends who expressed his amazement at Juha's strange demeanour and asked him, 'My friend, why don't you do as other people, and lay the saddle-bags on the donkey's back instead of carrying them on your own shoulders?'

'Don't you fear God?' replied Juha. 'Isn't it enough that this poor animal has to carry me, and yet you want him to carry the saddle-bags as well?'

Notes

1 The term *effendi* is a Turkish word which means 'mister'.
2 Based on an anecdote in *Laughable Stories* by Bar-Hebraeus, p. 166, translated and edited by E. A. Wallis Budge, Luzac & Co., London.
3 *Watad Juha.*

PART III

A SELECTION OF
ARAB PROVERBS

Everyone is content with their own intelligence.

The judge's sympathy is better than the testimony of two just witnesses.[1]

Who acts like a sheep will be eaten by wolves.

If you see a lion's teeth, do not take the sight for a smile.

The man who fears the lion least is the one who sees him most often.

The chameleon changes colour but remains a chameleon.

Do not teach the orphan to weep.

Have one eye open when you sell, and both when you buy.[2]

A little luck is better than a lot of wisdom.

If you shake hands with him, count your fingers first.

He kills the man, and attends his funeral.

One who is wet does not fear the rain.

She left her baby crying, and went to appease the neighbour's child.

Since the house is in ruins, why worry about the window?

Let the baker bake your bread, even though he might steal half of it.

He hit me and wailed, and then ran ahead of me and complained.

Starve your dog, and he will follow you; fatten him, and he will bite you.

If you want to marry, give your presents to the mother.

We taught him to beg, and he hastened before us to knock on the doors.

The fish ate the bait and smeared the hook with dirt.

He who receives the strokes of the cane is not like the one who counts them.

Like a sieve, he cannot keep a secret.

Who takes a crow as a guide will be led to the carcasses of dogs.

If the moon loves you, you need not worry about the stars.

Who plays with a cat must bear its claws.

When the camel falls, his butchers become numerous.

Whoever says what he should not will hear what he likes not.

Not every man who rides a horse is a horseman.

Eat what you please, but dress as others do.

Nothing will scratch your skin like your own nail.

Do not open a door that you cannot close.

A dog barks with greater fury in front of his own front door.

Better a wise man's enmity than a fool's friendship.

If the owl were good to eat the hunter would not have left it alone.

God will sometimes give chickpeas to one who has no teeth.

Whatever is brought by the winds is carried away by the storms.

A man talks less as his intelligence grows.

If you can find what you need in the market, do not solicit it from your brother.

Its guard is its thief.[3]

Information does not equal inspection.

Intelligence is the most precious of virtues, and ignorance the greatest of misfortunes.

A cat's dreams are all about mice.

Sometimes, silence constitutes an answer.

Novelty has its own appeal.

A hair from Satan's beard is indeed a prize.[4]

He is like a man who takes one step forward, and two steps back.

He cut off the tail of the snake, but left its head intact.

He who counsels a fool will become his enemy.

He who steals an egg will steal a camel.

He who has no backteeth should not attempt to chew hard food.

The farmer who is stingy in feeding his cat will have his corn eaten by mice.

Out of a few grains of sand he makes a dome.

He drowns himself in a few inches of water.

If you have to beg, knock on the rich man's door.

If you enter a village and find that its people worship the calf, then gather grass to feed the animal.

One who is bald does not need to curry favour with the barber.

He who knocks on the door will hear the answer.

We tell him: it is a bull, and he keeps saying, 'milk it'.

A screaming goat does not have its young eaten by the wolf.

Half a calamity is better than a whole disaster.

I taught him to steal and he slipped his hand in my pocket.

He gets a cake from every wedding.

They said to the one-eyed man, 'Blindness is hard.' He replied, 'I know half the story.'

The bald-headed woman brags about her niece's hair.

A madman threw a stone into a well, and a thousand men could not fetch it out.[5]

Worms attack only good wood.

Like one who attempts to carry water in a sieve.

Play for me on the drum, and I shall play for you on the flute.

Lament is the arm of the weak.

What is the use of patching up a worn-out robe?

The empty barrel resounds.

Don't throw stones into a well from which you drink.

The butcher is not frightened by the number of sheep.

Fear a man who does not fear God.

The saw will succeed where the hammer fails.

He who fears the devil will encounter him.

He who sails in a boat is not safe from drowning.

Even the snake charmer is not immune from snakebites.

We were two; where did the third come from?

An egg today is better than a chick tomorrow.

Throw him into the sea, and he will emerge with a fish in his mouth.

What has a beginning has also an end.

They wanted to teach the wolf the alphabet. They said 'A', he answered 'Goat'; they said 'B', he answered 'Kid'.

The misfortune of one nation can benefit another.

He consoles but he does not know who has died.

He is generous with the money of others.

A woman alone was able to wreck paradise.

The peacemaker often receives two-thirds of the blows.

If your friend is all sweetness, do not prey upon him all at once.

He is like the drum: he makes much noise, but is hollow inside.

Too many opinions obscure the truth.

As hungry as a louse on a bald head.

O God, deliver me from my friends. For my enemies, I'll take care of them myself.

The two litigants agree, and yet the judge objects.

A dead sheep feels not pain if it is skinned.

Peace between the cat and the mouse spells the grocer's ruin.

A wise man's doubt has more value than the certainty of a fool.

If I were to become an undertaker, no one would die.

Do not drink poison in reliance upon what you have acting as an antidote.

It is better to be afflicted by one who is completely mad than by one who is only half mad.

One cannot clap with one hand alone.

An empty rifle will frighten two men.[6]

The jealous eye brings out every fault, but the loving eye sees none.

He who makes of the wolf a shepherd commits an injustice to the sheep.

His excuse is more heinous than his crime.

Attempting to escape from the rain, he takes refuge under the water spout.

Do not trust a fool if he has a sword in his hand.

He who is not a wolf is likely to be eaten by wolves.

He hits me in the face and then asks the people, 'Why does he cry?'

The duckling floats.

The oppression of the cat is better than the justice of the mouse.

One whom you have accustomed to eating your food feels hungry whenever he sees you.

The lion never eats what is left over by the wolf.

Haste comes from the devil.

One should not scorn one's enemy, however feeble he might be, nor abandon one's caution, however insignificant he appears to be, for how often has a flea kept an elephant without sleep?

The wise men of Persia have said, 'It is better for a lion to lead a thousand foxes, than for a fox to lead a thousand lions.'

Do not stretch your legs beyond your rug.

A monkey is a gazelle in his mother's eyes.[7]

People will remain your friends until you become poor.

Do not buy the slave unless at the same time you also buy a stick.

Wherever the gloomy man goes, he is sure to meet a funeral.

If you cannot bite, do not show your teeth.

Happy is he who has no brain.

A guest is like fish: he stinks after three days.[8]

He gave him only the ear of the sheep.[9]

The devil does not ruin his own house.

A dog that barks does not bite.

Start screaming, and they will run away.

You are striking cold iron.

Beware of the harm that will befall you at the hands of one to whom you have been kind.

Love makes a man both blind and deaf.

Dissent, you will be remembered.

He is bald and still he wrangles about a comb!

Like one who blows into a leather bottle which has a hole in it.

Often a lamb attempts to teach its father how to graze.

Beware of where you place your confidence.

Choose the neighbour before you choose the house.

Play alone and you will win.

When one of two opponents comes to you with one eye lost, do not take his side until you have seen the other who may have lost both eyes.

Keep a vicious dog busy with a bone.

The world is on the side of he who is standing up.

He who leads the donkey to the top of the minaret will have to
bring it down.

The eloquent cock crows while still in the egg.

Man's worst enemy is his belly.

No misfortune is greater than one's own.

Everything forbidden is sweet.

The lion's den is not free of bones.

He would eat both the camel and its saddle.[10]

Each beard has its own comb.[11]

We opened the door for him, and he came in with his donkey.[12]

Men are not measured by the bushel.

One who plants thorns should not expect to pick roses.

No one belittles himself.

Advice given in public becomes criticism.

Punishment is of no value when the hair is grey.

The worthiest charity is that which is given before anything
is asked.

Stormy winds fell only the highest trees.

Women are like ribs: they snap if you try to straighten them.

If I have regretted once my silence, I have often lamented the fact of having spoken.

If the master of the house is fond of the tambourine, the whole family is given to dancing.

Like the camel who dies of thirst in the desert while carrying water on his back.

He travels free, and winks to the captain's wife.

Notes

1   The testimony of two just witnesses is a recognized proof under Islamic law.

2   Roman jurists expressed the second part of this saying by the legal maxim: *caveat emptor.*

3   This proverb is used to describe the theft of something by one who is charged with its protection. A similar idea was humorously expressed in a pharaonic caricature of ancient Egypt representing a wolf in the role of a shepherd of a herd of goats.

4   This saying means that a small benefit extracted from a miser is a great profit.

5   This means that a senseless act can sometimes lead to a disastrous situation.

6   It frightens the man against whom it is aimed as well as the man who, aiming it, knows the emptiness of his threat.

7   The Arabs consider the gazelle to be a symbol of grace and beauty.

8   Bedouin hospitality is proverbial, but its duration is customarily limited to three days: at the end of this period the guest is expected to take leave from his host and depart.

9   This proverb means that he took most of the profit.

10   This saying applies to a greedy man.

11   Means that different situations require different treatment.

12   Refers to an abuse of hospitality.

Bibliography

I. IN ARABIC

Al-Abshihi, *al-Mustatraf*, 2 vols, Cairo, 1942.

Arabsha', *Fakihat al-Khulafa'*, Cairo, 1290 AH.

Al-Asbahani, *Muhadarat al-Udaba'*, Beirut, 1961.

Al-Askari, *Jamharat al-Amthal*, 2 vols, Baghdad, 1964.

'Attri, A., *Adabuna al-Dahek*, Beirut.

Al-Balani, *Alef Ba'*.

Bustani, Ephrem, *al-Majani al-Haditha*, Beirut.

Farraj, Ahmed Abdel Sattar, *Akhbar Juha*, Cairo.

Al-Hamawi, *Thamarat al-Awraq*, Cairo, 1971.

Al-Hashimi, *Jawaher al-Adab*, 2 vols, Cairo, 1965.

Al-Houfi, *al-Fakihat fil Adab*, Cairo.

Al Hussari, *Thail Zahr al-Adab*, Cairo.

Ibn Abed Raddo, *al-'Iqd al-Fareed*, Cairo, 1913.

Ibn al-Jawzi, *Akhbar al-Hamqa*, Cairo, 1928.

Ibn al-Jawzi, *al-Azkiya'*, Damascus, 1971.

Ibn al-Muqaffa', *Kalilah and Dimnah*, Catholic Press, Beirut.

Ibn Mamati, *al-Fashoush fi Huqm Qaraqoash*, Cairo.

Ibn Qutaiba, *'Uyun al-Akhbar*, Cairo, 1952.

Al-Jahez, *al-Bayan wal Tabyeen*, 3 vols, Cairo, 1947.

Al-Jahez, *al-Hayawan*, 7 vols, Cairo, 1947.

Al-Mawsawi, *Nuzhat al-Jalees*, 2 vols, Cairo, 1293 AH.

Al-Mazini, Ibrahim Abdel Qader, *Soundouq al-Dunia*, Cairo.

Al-Midani, *Majma' al-Amthal*, 2 vols, Cairo, 1352 AH.

Al-Nawaji, *Halbat al-Kumait*, Cairo, 1276 Heg.

Al-Nuwairi, *Nihayat al-Arab*, Cairo, 1935.

Al-Qaliobi, *Nawader*, Cairo, 1953.

Al-Sharawani, *Hadiqat al-Afrah*, Cairo, 1302 AH.

Al-Sharawani, *Nafhat al-Yumn*, Calcutta edition, 1811.

Sheikho, Father Louis, *Majani al-Adab*, 4 vols, Catholic Press, Beirut.

Shikhani, Samir, *Kitab al-Uns*, Beirut, 1964.

Al-Tawheedi, *al-Basa'er wal Zhakha'er*, Damascus, 1964.

Al-Tawheedi, *al-Imta' wal Mu'anasa*, Beirut.

II. In English or French

Arberry, A. H., *Tales from the Masnavi*, Allen and Unwin, London, 1961.

Bar-Hebraeus, *Laughable Stories*, translated by E. A. W. Budge, Luzac & Co., 1897.

Basset, René, *Mille et un contes arabes*, 3 vols, Maisonneuve, Paris.

Burckhardt, J. L., *Arabic Proverbs*, Curzon Press, London.

Elwell-Sutton, L. P., *Persian Proverbs*, John Murray, London, 1954.

Feghali, Mgr. Michel, *Proverbes et dictons Syro-Libanais*, Paris, 1938.

Frayha Anis, *Modern Lebanese Proverbs*, Beirut, 1953.

Pellat, Charles, *The Life and Works of Jahez*, Routledge and Kegan Paul, London, 1969.

Siavash-Danesh, *An Anthology of Persian Prose*, Vahid Publishing Co., Teheran, 1971.

Index of Stories